THE NUN

DENIS DIDEROT was born at Langres in eastern France in 1713, the son of a master cutler. He was originally destined for the Church but rebelled and persuaded his father to allow him to complete his education in Paris, where he graduated in 1732. For ten years Diderot was nominally a law student, but actually led a precarious bohemian but studious existence, eked out with tutoring, hack writing and translating. His original works, *Pensées philosophiques* (1746), *Lettre sur les aveugles* (1749) and *De l'interprétation de la nature* (1753), display a preoccupation with the mind-body dichotomy. In the early 1740s, however, he had met three contemporaries of great future significance for himself and for the age: d'Alembert, Condillac and J. J. Rousseau, who were to assist him in the compilation of the *Encyclopédie*, which Diderot edited right up to its completion in 1773. His boldest philosophical and scientific speculations are brilliantly summarized in a trilogy of dialogues: *Entretien entre Diderot et d'Alembert*, *Le rêve de d'Alembert* (*d'Alembert's Dream*) and *Suite de l'entretien* (1769). In *Le neveu de Rameau* (*Rameau's Nephew*), written in 1761 or later, he gave to prose fiction a new creative scope. Towards the end of his life he visited St Petersburg at the invitation of Catherine II, to whom he bequeathed his library. He died in 1784.

LEONARD TANCOCK spent most of his life in or near London, apart from a year as a student in Paris, most of the Second World War in Wales, and three periods in American universities as visiting professor. Until his death in 1986, he was a Fellow of University College, London, and was formerly Reader in French at the University. He prepared his first Penguin Classic in 1949 and, from that time, was extremely interested in the problems of translation, about which he wrote, lectured and gave broadcasts. His numerous translations for the Penguin Classics include Zola's *Germinal*, *Thérèse Raquin*, *The Débâcle*, *L'Assommoir* and *La Bête Humaine*; Diderot's *The Nun*, *Rameau's Nephew* and *D'Alembert's Dream*; Maupassant's *Pierre and Jean*; Marivaux's *Up from the Country*; Constant's *Adolphe*; La Rochefoucauld's *Maxims*; Voltaire's *Letters on England*; Prévost's *Manon Lescaut*; and Madame de Sévigné's *Selected Letters*.

DENIS DIDEROT

THE NUN

Translated from the French
with an introduction by
Leonard Tancock

PENGUIN BOOKS

PENGUIN BOOKS

Published by the Penguin Group
Penguin Books Ltd, 80 Strand, London WC2R 0RL, England
Penguin Putnam Inc., 375 Hudson Street, New York, New York 10014, USA
Penguin Books Australia Ltd, 250 Camberwell Road, Camberwell, Victoria 3124, Australia
Penguin Books Canada Ltd, 10 Alcorn Avenue, Toronto, Ontario, Canada M4V 3B2
Penguin Books India (P) Ltd, 11 Community Centre, Panchsheel Park, New Delhi – 110 017, India
Penguin Books (NZ) Ltd, Cnr Rosedale and Airborne Roads, Albany, Auckland, New Zealand
Penguin Books (South Africa) (Pty) Ltd, 24 Sturdee Avenue, Rosebank 2196, South Africa

Penguin Books Ltd, Registered Offices: 80 Strand, London WC2R 0RL, England

www.penguin.com

First published by Folio Society 1972
Published in Penguin Books 1974
26

Copyright © The Folio Society Ltd, 1972
All rights reserved

Printed in England by Clays Ltd, St Ives plc
Set in Linotype Georgian

www.greenpenguin.co.uk

Penguin Books is committed to a sustainable future
for our business, our readers and our planet.
The book in your hands is made from paper
certified by the Forest Stewardship Council.

To Mario

Si on me presse de dire pourquoy je l'aymois, je sens que cela ne se peut exprimer, qu'en respondant: Par ce que c'estoit luy; par ce que c'estoit moy.

L.W.T.

Introduction

Introduction

Denis Diderot (1713–84) is in many ways the most human and attractive of the three great figures in eighteenth-century French literature. As writers Voltaire and Rousseau are of course, each in his way, greater, but as men they have their limitations and are a little inhuman and sometimes even repellent. Diderot was broader in his interests than either and scarcely less deep, his critical insight was unclouded by envy and spite. His humanity and breadth of interests come from his dual nature. On the one side he is a scientific materialist, an atheist whose scheme of things reduces all human activity to the laws of chemistry, physics and physiology, but on the other, and in equal degree, he is an emotional and artistic type, with an intense belief in moral values and the blessed gift of tears. In an undated fragment of a letter to his friend and confidant Sophie Volland he confesses to this eternal duality within himself – a duality so often expressed in his works by the dialogue form: 'It infuriates me to be enmeshed in a devilish philosophy which my mind is forced to accept but my heart to disown.' In a word, he is the most complete expression of the eighteenth-century dilemma: the contradiction between scientific determinism and sentimental faith in the social virtues.

As editor for over twenty years of the *Encyclopédie*, the first great modern work of reference, Diderot is the supreme figure of the Enlightenment, but alongside this immense activity he was writing some philosophical treatises and dialogues at that time almost terrifying in their anti-religious implications, some rather ponderous and unsuccessful plays, full of sentiment and virtue, but some brilliant dramatic criticism, a series of *Salons*, the first great examples of that peculiarly French genre, art criticism as a form of literature, and one or two works of fiction, or rather events or philosophical debates fictionalized. These novels, if such they can be called, were not to be published for many years, and some of them not in Diderot's lifetime, but were circulated among his intimates. It is arguable that these unpublished works, especially *Le Neveu de Rameau* and *Le Rêve de D'Alembert*, express the real Diderot, a man far more advanced in his opinions on materialism, religious, moral and sexual emancipation than he could ever have shown himself to be in his 'official' writings, which had to withstand the relentless hostility of the establishment of the day, armed with the censorship, which several times jeopardized the publication of the *Encyclopédie* itself. Of these personal works the one which most clearly comes from the heart and which at the same time comes nearest to being a disciplined, organized novel, even a great work of art, is *La Religieuse*. And this began as a hoax.

The Marquis de Croismare, with whose name the novel opens, was a real person, a pious, sincere Catholic, charitable and kind, but he was also a member of the circle of friends consisting of such 'Encyclopedists' as Madame d'Epinay, F. M. Grimm and Diderot, and they were very fond of him. This incidentally shows the common sense and broadmindedness of so many people of intelligence at that time. It is a gross over-simplification to suppose that in eighteenth-century France, even during the sometimes fierce Encyclopedic war, everybody automatically hated either the Catholics or the Freethinkers. Many people were capable of human friendships transcending ideological or religious opinion. Today we seem to be less fortunate. In 1758 M. de Croismare interested himself in a *cause célèbre*. A nun in the Paris convent of Longchamp was appealing to be dispensed from her vows and to be allowed to return into the world. Croismare used his influence in her favour, but without success. He never met her personally; his conduct was motivated solely by sympathy for a poor woman trying to extricate herself from a life of misery to which she had been condemned by her parents. This nun, Marguerite Delamarre, lost her case in March 1758 and was forced to remain in religious orders for the rest of her life.

Less than a year later Croismare, a nobleman from Normandy who had spent much of his time in Paris, decided, since he was now well on in his sixties, to retire to his castle of Lasson, near Caen. He was sadly missed by his circle of friends. Whereupon they hatched a plot to lure him back to Paris by appealing to his kind heart. They pretended that a young nun had escaped from her convent, that she was at present in hiding at the home in Versailles of another member of the group, a Madame Moreau-Madin, to whom all correspondence should be addressed. Madame Madin was known to all parties, and the conspirators arranged for her to hand over to them letters franked from Caen.

The elaborate practical joke began early in 1760. Letters supposedly written by the escaped nun or by Madame Madin herself, but composed by Diderot, were sent via Versailles, letters in which the wretched girl begged Croismare to help her. But almost at once the joke got seriously out of control in two ways.

Firstly, the Marquis showed no signs of wanting to hasten back to Paris, but his expressions of sympathy and offers of help were so immediate that Diderot could hardly believe he was so gullible, and in a letter to Madame d'Epinay on 10 February he feared that Croismare had seen through the plot and was double-bluffing. The kind Croismare was soon offering to find a position for the ex-nun in his own household, and Diderot had to use delaying tactics in the form of letters describing the girl's impaired state of health which would prevent her travelling. But by the end of March the helpful gentleman was offering to arrange for Suzanne Simonin – the nun's name – to take the Caen coach, and detailed instructions were being sent. By April the plotters were getting into very deep water, and clearly the only way out was to kill off the unfortunate nun and put an end to the whole business. Accordingly letters ostensibly from Madame Madin were sent describing the terrible illness and last sufferings of the poor girl, culminating in a touching letter dated 10 May describing her death: 'The dear child is no more; her sufferings are at an end, but ours may still last a long time. She passed from this world into the one whither we all are bound, last Wednesday between three and four in the morning...' etc.

But secondly the joke got out of hand in a way that produced one of the most remarkable novels of the eighteenth century, for the real sufferings of Marguerite Delamarre and the fictitious ones of Suzanne Simonin took possession of Diderot's own imagination, and with his usual single-mindedness he threw himself into a complete story of Suzanne's life, from childhood to her present plight. Clearly this would have to be in autobiographical form, which at once meant that the nun must still be alive after the end of the story, and indeed, as we know from his correspondence, Diderot was working on *La Religieuse* all through the summer of 1760, that is long after the account of her death sent to M. de Croismare. The novel, like so many other Diderot texts, was not published. However, in 1768, M. de Croismare came to Paris and saw his old friend Madame Madin who, to his great surprise, was clearly unfamiliar with certain colourful episodes, accounts of which, ostensibly from her, had been sent to him eight years before. So the whole story came out.

As there was now no reason for secrecy about the conspiracy, Grimm published, in 1770, in the *Correspondance Littéraire* (the periodical circulated to a very small but highly privileged list of subscribers throughout Europe, including Catherine of Russia) an account of the whole story and the text of the letters in the exchanges of 1760. The mere fact that this *Préface-Annexe*, as it was called, was published, however privately, and a hint in the last letter that the hapless nun had left behind her some account of her earlier life, suggested that further revelations might come at some future time. In 1780 the *Correspondance Littéraire*, no longer edited by Grimm but by Meister, needed copy, and with Diderot's consent the text was copied and sent to the very small circle of subscribers. This was the only text published in Diderot's lifetime.

Then came the Revolution and with it, of course, a change of climate concerning books previously held to be dangerous or subversive. The Directory would obviously welcome exposures of the abuses of the Old Régime. The first proper printed edition appeared in 1796, and it was translated within a year into German, Italian and English.

Real life has its untidinesses and illogicalities, art has its own truth to which it must be faithful. So when Diderot the novelist was presenting the case for a woman without a religious vocation enclosed against her will in an unnatural environment, he instinctively concentrated events, eliminated factors not bearing directly upon the case, introduced elements calculated to make things more acceptable to the general reader, just as a dramatist must do when he makes a play out of some real-life story.

The object of the attack is enforced and unnatural segregation of people of the same sex in an institution, with all its dehumanizing effects. It is not an attack upon Christianity, or even the Catholic Church, which is no doubt why the Church never put it on the *Index*, as it did many other works of Diderot, and those of Voltaire *en bloc*. Sister Suzanne's faith never leaves her, and there are one or two wholly admirable Christian characters. The tone throughout is respectful of sincere religion. The attack is against misconceived Christianity applied by ignorant, warped and unnatural people in a social system where the civil law protects the persecutor and penalizes the victim. At that time in France the age at which binding religious vows could be taken was regulated by the state at sixteen and release from them could only be granted by the state. In 1768 Louis XV, under pressure, raised this age to eighteen. When it is remembered that the legal majority for disposing of one's own money was twenty-five, the anomaly is seen to be absurd. Thus in this novel Suzanne, under irresistible pressure, could legally dispose of herself, body and soul, for ever at the age of sixteen, but have no say in her money affairs, being still under twenty-five. Now the story of Marguerite Delamarre, who may be regarded as the prototype of Suzanne, was in some respects untypical and unnecessarily complicated. She was over forty when she lost her case, and had been boarded out in various institutions from earliest childhood by a mother who had never wanted her and a miserly father who resented having to pay any money for her, and who had broken off an engagement when the girl was sixteen, presumably because the cheapest convent he could find cost far less money than a marriage dowry. It is true that financial considerations count in the case of Diderot's Suzanne, but the root cause of her incarceration is that she is illegitimate. Her mother regarded her as a constant reproach, and her mother's husband knew the circumstances of her birth and loathed the child. Her mother's selfish and ignorant idea of atoning for her sin was to make her child into a sacrificial offering in order to gain *her own* salvation. Moreover the psychological and artistic disadvantage of having a suffering victim of over forty was avoided by making Suzanne very young, sensitive and intelligent. Finally, in choosing the elements to be taken out of the real life story of Marguerite Delamarre, Diderot eliminates any reference to the real person's early engagement to be married, which was forcibly broken by her father. Artistically and psychologically this has the great advantage of concentrating and simplifying the thesis of the book, for by so doing Diderot makes it clear that in no case is abnormality a result of any 'normal' but unfortunate sexual experience *with a man*. These women (especially the Superior) are not what they are because in youth they have been deeply shocked or warped by such things as disgust, violence or even frustrated, unhappy love.

The resulting novel is by no means a flawless work of art. Its great interest lies in its atmosphere and power and in Diderot's struggles and relative success in overcoming the technical difficulties of his self-imposed task. Not only the circumstances of the original hoax but also the psycho-

logical necessities of the novel impose a narrative in the first
person by the heroine, who must be young and impressionable throughout her story. The first trouble therefore is
that too many adventures have to be crowded into a short
time. But that in itself is but the inevitable concentration of
all art. More serious is the improbable treatment of time in
relation to psychological growth and the lessons of experience. In order to give sustained interest Suzanne has to be
subjected to a series of trials of increasing severity. But this
very fact that she must be afflicted afresh with new and
more acute fear and anguish means that she must remain
throughout the innocent victim in spite of the manifest
presence around her of evil and perversion, and this with
her obvious intelligence and in a tale told retrospectively by
a narrator perfectly aware of the end. Of course her quasi-
miraculous preservation may be attributed to the protecting
presence of God, but the question of character cannot altogether be avoided. She remains sweet and kind even to those
who torture her, and she does not forget to point this out
with a certain smugness. She is wonderfully observant, with
Diderot's eye for the characteristic gesture or facial expression, but in spite of all her experience, including having
been accused of masturbation or homosexual practices, she
is completely innocent and uncomprehending in the face of
the homosexual approaches of the Superior of Sainte-
Eutrope. It is true that the evolution of the Superior from a
kindly, if somewhat scatterbrained and comic, person to a
sinister Lesbian is beautifully graded, but it is stretching
credibility to breaking point to make Suzanne quite unaware of the meaning of her Superior's behaviour when it
comes to describing an orgasm in almost clinical detail. One
is tempted to compare these passages with the classical
method of so much frankly pornographic literature: narra-
tion by a young girl of what somebody did to her in terms
combining innocence with extreme accuracy of physical
description.

But it would be wrong to accuse Diderot of simple negli-
gence or *naïveté*. The truth is that he was always so in-

volved, mind and heart, in what he was doing at any given time, that he could see it happening and for the time being he was the character he was portraying. Nowhere is this more clear than in his capricious use of tenses, for so often Suzanne refers to an event or person in a continuous present tense, even when that person's death has already been reported. There is, for example, the terrible muddle over Sister Ursule. Suzanne urges her correspondent, M. de Croismare, to be very prudent because Sister Ursule is still alive, but then she remembers that she is dead, and apologizes for her slip by saying that at least that is what she had told him before. But there was no 'before', since she was writing for the first time. The truth is that Diderot, in his creative trance, lives in the eternal vivid present of the world of dreams, outside time, and we have to live with Suzanne as though it were all happening now, before our eyes.

If further proof were needed of Diderot's capacity for losing himself in what he is doing at the moment, one could point out that in a different mood, when he is writing *Jacques le Fataliste*, Diderot will pour withering scorn on the inconsistencies, improbabilities and lack of physical or psychological realism in most of the novels of his age. But then he will be concerned with the mechanics of the novel, now he is concerned with a poor girl's sufferings.

Although by the time he was writing the novel as we now know it the original trick on Croismare had been abandoned, Diderot clearly felt that his tale would be unacceptable unless it played itself out in a plausible setting. Croismare knew his Paris, and in any case the great Paris convents were known very well by everybody, inside and out. Not only were they virtually the only educational institutions for girls, but in some cases parts of the buildings were let off in apartments to fashionable people. It is one of the amusing ironies of eighteenth-century Paris life that one of the greatest salons in Europe, and the very hotbed of rationalist and anti-religious talk, was that of Madame du Deffand in her two-storey apartment in the convent of

Saint-Joseph in the rue Saint-Dominique, frequented by everybody from Voltaire and Montesquieu to Jean-Jacques Rousseau (when not in one of his sulks). Significantly enough that convent had been founded by Madame de Montespan. Moreover several of those fashionable convents were famous for the quality of their music, and crowds attended the services with full choral and orchestral Masses and other more or less 'sacred' music, as indeed elsewhere in Europe they heard the church music of Haydn and Mozart. In Paris these were treated as concerts, and the audiences even applauded the singers. The musical talent of Suzanne and her success in public performances is therefore part of the strict realism of the setting. Not that this is the only realism, for Diderot has an infallible eye for personal appearance, gesture and mannerisms, grouping and lighting effects that make some of his scenes as unforgettable as a Dutch painting. Indeed it might be said that *La Religieuse* has no literary ancestry at all except the dramatic work of Diderot and his art criticism. Diderot's manipulation of light and shade, with darkness relieved only by candlelight or the faint glimmer of altar-lamps, sets the scene for these lives of claustrophobic unhealthiness, mental instability, illness, anxiety and febrile intensity.

It might be said that life in any closed institution tends to be over-intense, full of gossip and triviality, factions, intrigues, favouritism, persecutions and pettiness, in a word subject to the exaggerated reactions of mass-psychology, and that power corrupts, especially the power of women in authority over other women. And all that might equally be found in a boarding school or in those modern relics of the monastic system, the great hospitals. But in a convent, where the inmates are, so to speak, serving a life sentence in the service of God, there are no holidays, mitigations, changes of scene – or not until the very recent 'liberalization' of religious orders. Diderot sees four kinds of danger in the segregated life, and these correspond to the successive experiences of Suzanne Simonin. They are madness, the paralysing effect of a saintly, mystical personality who inspires blind hero-worship, sadistic cruelty and bullying, and homosexuality, which can include elements of the other three. The first three of these manifestations of unbalance in an artificial society call for no elaboration, but Diderot's treatment of the fourth is remarkable for its period. Hitherto homosexual behaviour had been considered either an unspeakable abomination in the eyes of God and man or, alternatively, one of the two or three eternal themes of pornography. Few had treated it objectively and still fewer with any attempt at sympathy or understanding. Diderot does both.

From the beginning of his career he had been deeply interested in every aspect of medical science, and in particular in the inter-dependence of the physical and so-called spiritual phenomena of human life, and this of course had led him to the suggestion that morality is not an absolute thing, but relative and always a purely *social* matter. A man cannot be immoral alone on a desert island. Which will lead Diderot, notably in *Le Rêve de D'Alembert*, to strike an astonishingly modern note in his plea for common sense and tolerance where some kinds of deviant sexual behaviour are concerned. Before condemning an act as criminal, he asks, would it not be wise to look into the environment?

But his genuine scientific interest and single-minded absorption in the question of the moment can lead Diderot into literary and artistic improbabilities, for the minute description of the Superior's behaviour in states of sexual excitement does strike at the very roots of truth and realism as he preaches them in some of his critical writings. Such accuracy on the part of a girl who was not supposed to understand may be realism in one narrow sense, but it is anything but realistic coming from a narrator who, we are frequently reminded, had no idea what was going on until the scales fell from her eyes when she overheard the Superior's confession.

Diderot's originality lies elsewhere. Instead of the conventional reactions of pious horror or dirty sniggering, his is a bold assertion that homosexuality is a temperamental condition intensified and made active by unnatural environment. So far this is unexceptionable. But where he is inconsistent, and surely in error from a modern point of view, is in his revelation (suggested perhaps by remnants of conventional timidity) that the Mother Superior had been more or less insane all along, which of course undermines his thesis about segregation and environment. And given all this, what are we to conclude about the wretched woman's agonizing remorse and death, which are presumably the punishment for her sin? Possibly that it was a convenient way of ending the story, yet even this apparent illogicality is part and parcel of Diderot's unfailing humanity, for the final impression is that this woman is not a repulsive monster of perversion, but a poor soul to be pitied, another victim of the evil system. It is this same human sympathy which prompts what might be thought the one serious lapse from good taste in this novel. After all her ordeals, which Diderot develops with delicacy and good taste, he allows his nun to be helped to escape by her second confessor, Dom Morel, who promptly assaults her sexually in the cab he has hired for the purpose. This appears to let the story down from a cautionary tale to the level of the traditional bawdy tale about the priest and the young nun. But even here Suzanne's narrative makes it clear that Dom Morel, too, had been put as a youth with no vocation and against his will into the monastic life for which he was quite unsuited. He is as much a victim and product of the system as anybody else, and Suzanne's last word about him when she hears that he has been recaptured and forcibly taken back is one of infinite pity.

A recent French film of the novel, for a long time banned in France by the De Gaulle government, ended by showing Suzanne, lured into the brothel, break away from a man's lewd embraces and hurl herself from a window to her death on the pavement below. Nothing could be more wrong, for the really sinister thing about *La Religieuse* is its inconclusive ending. With masterly economy and one of his flashes of genius, Diderot cuts Suzanne's continuous narrative short at a point where there is nothing more to be said about the main theme, and by tacking on what purport to be rough notes Diderot indicates some of the possible developments that most other eighteenth-century novelists, with their love of episodes, flashbacks and digressions, would have found irresistible, however irrelevant. A Lesage, a Marivaux, a Restif de la Bretonne, even a Rousseau, would probably have told us the parallel life of Dom Morel, the early histories of some of the nuns, and much more besides. Moreover, in these rough notes Diderot uses his stylistic trick of darting to and fro between the present and past tenses not merely in order to be vivid and arresting, as earlier in the novel, but with telling artistic and psychological effect, to express Suzanne's distress and confusion. Incidents in her past have been so traumatic that to her they are still the terrible present. That is why in this translation I have respected Diderot's deliberate muddle and not attempted to 'edit' him, for it serves to show that his poor heroine is cut off from the world of practical reality. After her years of convent life she is unsuited for anything, a lost, helpless soul with no knowledge, no skill except some music, no initiative, no future. Her life is so empty and hopeless that she is tempted to go back to the convent. Real tragedy consists not in death but in having nothing to live for.

LEONARD TANCOCK

Hertford, 1972.

Translator's Note. Technical terms in connection with convent life and nuns' attire vary according to the orders. Diderot gives no indication of this and the story is two hundred years old. I have therefore used the most general terms, after some discussion with both French and English Catholics, including a nun.

Introduction

The text used for this translation is that in: Diderot: *Oeuvres romanesques*, ed. H. Bénac, Classiques Garnier, Paris 1951, and subsequent reprints. The only full-scale study of the novel is in French: Georges May, *Diderot et 'La Religieuse'*, 1954. The following books in English will be found helpful and interesting:

John Lough, *An Introduction to Eighteenth-Century France*, London, Longmans, 1960.
Robert Niklaus, 'The Eighteenth Century 1715–1789' in *A Literary History of France*, London, Benn, 1970.
Vivienne Mylne, *The Eighteenth-Century French Novel*, Manchester University Press, 1965.

L.W.T.

The Nun

The Marquis de Croismare's reply, if he does reply, will serve as the opening lines of this tale. Before writing to him I wanted to know what he was like. He is a man of the world, he has had a distinguished military career, is elderly, a widower with a daughter and two sons whom he loves and who return his affection. He is well born, enlightened, intelligent and witty, is fond of the arts and above all has an original mind. I have had enthusiastic accounts of his sensitivity, honour and probity, and I have learned from the keen interest he has taken in this affair of mine, and from everything I have been told, that I was running no risks at all by confiding in him. But that is no reason why he should resolve to reshape my destiny without knowing who I am, and it is for this reason that I have made up my mind to overcome my pride and reluctance and embark on these recollections in which I shall describe part of my misfortunes without talent or artifice, with the ingenuousness of a girl of my age and with my natural candour. Since my benefactor might require it, or perhaps the spirit might move me to finish these memoirs at a time when distant events had faded from my memory, I thought that the summary at the end, as well as the profound impression I shall keep as long as I live, would suffice to bring them back to my mind with accuracy.

My father was an advocate. He had married my mother rather late in life and they had three daughters. He had more than enough money to settle all three comfortably, but that supposed at any rate an equal share of love for them, and that is the last thing I can give him credit for. Certainly I surpassed my sisters in qualities of mind and beauty, character and ability, and this seemed to upset my parents. As my natural and acquired advantages over them only brought sorrow to me, I strove from my very earliest days to be like them in the hope of being loved, cherished, indulged and excused as they were. If anybody happened to say to my mother: 'Your children are charming', it was never taken as referring to me. Sometimes this wrong was more than righted, but such praises as I then received were so cruelly paid for when we were alone that I would just as soon have met indifference or even insults, for the more the visitors had shown preference for me the more unkindly was I treated when they had gone. Oh, how many times I wept because I was not born ugly, foolish, silly, conceited, in a word with all the disadvantages that served the others so well with our parents! I wondered what could be the reason for this strange behaviour in a father and mother otherwise good, fair-minded and pious. Shall I tell you? Odd words let slip by my father when in a temper, for he was a choleric man, and certain happenings over the years – words dropped by neighbours, things said by servants – made me suspect a reason which might excuse them a little. Perhaps my father had his doubts about my birth, possibly I reminded my mother of an indiscretion and the baseness of a man to whom she had been too soft-hearted, how can I say? But even if these suspicions were unfounded, what risk would there be in my passing them on to you? You will burn this letter, and I promise to burn your answers.

As all three of us were very close to each other in age we all grew up together. Eligible young suitors appeared. My eldest sister was courted by a charming young man, but before long I realized that he was more interested in me, and I guessed that very soon she would only be the pretext for his repeated visits. I foresaw all the trouble this preference might bring upon me, and I warned my mother. That was perhaps the only thing I have done in my whole life that pleased her, and this is how I was rewarded. Four days, or anyway only a few days later, I was told that a place had been arranged for me in a convent, and the very next day I was taken there. Life at home was so miserable that this did not upset me, and I went off to Sainte-Marie, my first convent, in high spirits. As for my sister's young man, I was out of sight and out of mind, and he duly married her. His name is Monsieur K., he is a lawyer living in Corbeil, and his home life is very unhappy indeed. My second sister was married to a Monsieur Bauchon, a Paris silk merchant in the rue Quincampoix, and they get on fairly well together.

As my sisters were married off, I thought I should be remembered and soon be out of the convent. I was then sixteen and a half. My sisters had been given considerable dowries, I expected similar treatment, and my head was full of the delightful things I was going to do, when I was summoned to the parlour. It was Father Séraphin, my mother's confessor and formerly mine as well, and without any beating about the bush he came at once to the object of his visit, which was to persuade me to take the veil. I protested at this strange proposal and made it quite clear that I was not in the least drawn towards the religious life. 'That is a pity,' he said, 'for your parents have spent everything on your sisters, and I cannot see what they could possibly do for you in the impoverished position they have come down to. Think it over, Mademoiselle; either you must enter this house forever or go away to some provincial convent where they will take you in for a modest fee, and you will not leave it until the death of your parents, which may not happen for a long time.' I lamented bitterly, and shed floods of tears. The Mother Superior had been informed and was waiting for me when I returned from the parlour. My distress was indescribable. She said: 'What's the matter with you, my child (knowing even better than I did what was the matter), what a state you're in! Really, there never was such despair, you make me shudder! Have you lost your father or your mother?' As I threw myself into her arms I very nearly said: 'I wish to God I had!' but I merely cried out: 'Alas, I have no father or mother, I am a poor, wretched creature they detest and want to bury alive in this place.' She let the storm die down and waited for calm to be

restored. Then I explained more clearly just what I had
been told. She appeared to be sorry for me, sympathized
and encouraged me not to take up a calling for which I had
no vocation, and she promised to pray, remonstrate and
appeal. Oh, Sir, you have no conception of the deceitful
wiles of these Superiors of convents. She did write, knowing
perfectly well the sort of replies she would get; she passed
them on to me, and it was some time before I began to
suspect her good faith. However, the time allowed for me to
make up my mind came to an end, and she came to tell me
the outcome, with the most carefully calculated sadness.
First she remained silent, then uttered a few words of sympathy from which I gathered what the rest would be. There
was another scene of despair, and I shall not have many
more to describe. Self-control is the great art of these
people. Then she said, and I really think with genuine
tears: 'Well, my child, so you are going to leave us! Dear
child, we shall never see each other again!' – and so forth.
But I didn't take it in. I was slumped in a chair, I either said
nothing or sobbed, stayed motionless or jumped up, went
and supported myself against the wall or poured forth my
grief on her bosom. After all this she went on to say: 'But
why don't you do one thing? Listen, but do please mind
you don't say I gave you this advice – I am relying on your
absolute discretion over this, for I wouldn't for anything in
the world want to incur any criticism. What do they want
you to do? Take the veil? Well, why don't you? What does
it commit you to? Nothing, except staying another two
years with us here. We are here today and gone tomorrow;
two years is quite a time, and many things can happen in
two years...' With these insidious arguments she threw in
so many caresses, so many protestations of friendship, so
many affectionate falsehoods, such as I knew where I was
now but not where I might be taken, that I let myself be
persuaded. So she wrote to my father, and a very fine letter
it was, oh yes, a better one you couldn't have found –
neither my pain and grief nor pleas were concealed – a far
cleverer girl than me would have been taken in, I assure

you. And so my consent was given and that settled that. How expeditiously everything was made ready! The day was fixed, my habit prepared, the hour for the ceremony had come, and looking back now I cannot see the slightest interval between these events.

I forgot to mention that I saw my father and mother and did all in my power to touch their hearts, but found them adamant. The exhortation was pronounced by a certain Abbé Blin, Doctor of the Sorbonne, and the Bishop of Aleppo gave me the habit. This ceremony is hardly gay in itself, but that day it was as gloomy as can be. Although the nuns were full of attentions in giving me their support, my knees seemed to be giving way a score of times and I felt myself on the point of collapsing on the altar steps. I heard nothing, saw nothing and was quite dazed. I went where I was led, I was questioned and they answered for me. Yet the cruel ceremony eventually came to an end, the people all went away and I stayed with the flock to which I had been consigned. My companions surrounded me, embraced me, saying to each other: 'Just look, Sister, isn't she lovely! How this black veil brings out the whiteness of her skin! How well that band suits her! How it rounds off her face and cheeks! How well her habit shows off her figure and arms!' I scarcely took in what they were saying, for I was overcome with grief. And yet I must confess that when I was alone in my cell I recalled their flattering remarks and couldn't resist verifying them in my little mirror, and I felt they were not altogether undeserved. There are special honours belonging to this day, and they were exaggerated in my case but I scarcely noticed, though they pretended to think just the opposite, and told me so, which clearly was not true. That evening after prayers the Superior came into my cell. 'Really,' she said, after looking me up and down, 'I don't know why you have such an objection to the habit; it suits you perfectly and you look charming. Sister Suzanne is a very lovely nun, and she will be all the more popular for that. Now let's see you walk along. You're not holding yourself quite straight, you mustn't stoop like that...' She placed my head, hands and feet, body and arms, and it was almost like one of Marcel's dancing lessons on convent graces, for there are some for every walk in life. Then she took a seat and said: 'All right, but now let us talk seriously. We have gained two years. Your parents may change their minds, you yourself may want to stay here when they want to take you away – that would be by no means impossible.' 'No, Madame, don't you believe it.' 'You have been with us a long time, but you have no idea yet what our life is like; it may have its sorrows, but it also has its joys.' You have a good idea of the sort of thing she was certain to have gone on to say about the world and the cloister, for it is written everywhere and in just the same way. For, thank God, I had had to read the piles of rubbish that monks and nuns have produced about their way of life, which they know inside out and loathe, against the world that they love, tear to pieces but don't know.

I won't go into details about my novitiate. If one observed all its austerities one would never survive, yet it is the pleasantest period of monastic life. A novice-mistress is always the most indulgent sister who can be found. Her object is to hide from you all the thorns of the vocation, she subjects you to a course of the most carefully calculated seduction. Her function is to darken still more the shades of night which surround you, to lull you into slumber, to throw dust in your eyes, to fascinate you, and ours paid special attention to me. I don't believe there exists a single young and inexperienced soul who is proof against this terrible art. There are pitfalls out in the world, but I don't imagine you reach them down such a gentle slope. I had only to sneeze twice and I was excused from religious observances, work and prayer. I went to bed earlier and rose later, the whole rule was waived for me. Just fancy, Sir, there were times when I actually longed for the day when I should make the final sacrifice. Not a single unsavoury story happens in the world outside without your being told about it, and the true stories are revised and false ones are invented, on top of which endless praises are sung and acts of thanksgiving made to God who shelters us from these humiliating adventures. Meanwhile the day I had sometimes wished to hurry on was drawing near, and then I became thoughtful and felt my distaste coming back more strongly than ever. I went either to the Mother Superior or to our novice-mistress and confided in them. These women are well compensated for the trouble you give them, for one cannot suppose that they enjoy the hypocritical part they play and the nonsense they are forced to say over and over again. It all gets so repetitious and boring for them, but they face up to it for the sake of the thousand crowns their house makes out of it. That is the vital aim for which they spend a lifetime of deceit and prepare for innocent young girls forty or fifty years of despair and probably an eternity of suffering, for it is a certain fact, Sir, that out of every hundred nuns who die before fifty there are exactly one hundred damned, and that taking no account of the ones who in the meantime lose their reason, get feeble-minded or go raving mad.

There came a day when one of these last escaped from the cell where she was shut up. I saw her. That was the beginning of my good or bad fortune – according, Sir, to how you treat me henceforth. I have never seen anything so horrible. She was all dishevelled and half naked, she was dragging iron chains, wild-eyed, tearing her hair and beating her breast, rushing along and shrieking. She was heaping upon herself and everyone else the most appalling curses, and looking for a window to throw herself out of. I was seized with panic and trembled in every limb, seeing my own fate in that of this unhappy creature, and thereupon a vow was made in my heart that I would die a thousand deaths rather than expose myself to it. They realized the effect this event might have on my mind and that it must be forestalled. So I was told all manner of ridiculous and contradictory lies about this nun, such as that her mind was already deranged when she was admitted, that she had had a terrible shock at a critical stage of her development, she was given to seeing visions, she thought she was in communication with the angels, she had read some pernicious books which had turned her brain, she had listened to the inventors of a new and outlandish moral code who had made her so terrified of the judgement of God that her already weakened mind had given way, she now saw nothing but demons, hell and fiery abysses; and they were most unfortunate, for it was unheard of that there had ever been anyone like that in their house before – and heaven knows what else besides. It didn't work on me. My demented nun constantly haunted my mind and I constantly swore to myself that I would never take any vow.

But soon the moment had come for showing whether I could keep the promise I had made to myself. One morning after service the Superior came to see me. She had a letter in her hand. Her face expressed misery and grief, her arms hung loose and it seemed as though her hand couldn't find the strength to hold up the letter. As she looked at me tears seemed to flow from her eyes, she said not a word and neither did I; she was waiting for me to speak first, but I resisted the temptation. So she asked me how I was, saying that office had been very long that day, I had coughed a bit and she thought I might not be feeling well. All this I answered with: 'No, dear Mother.' She still held the letter in a drooping hand, but in the middle of these questions she put it down on her lap, partially concealed by her hand. At length, having skirted round the subject by asking various questions about my father and mother, she realized that I was not going to ask her what the paper was, and so said: 'Here is a letter . . .'

This made my heart miss a beat, and it was with faltering voice and trembling lips that I completed the sentence: '. . . from my mother?'

'As you say. Here you are, read it.'

I recovered a little, took the letter which at first I read fairly steadily, but as I went on fear, indignation, anger, vexation, one passion after another possessed me, and I had different voices, took on different expressions and made different gestures. At one moment I could scarcely hold the

paper, at another I gripped it as if to tear it in pieces, or
grasped it fiercely as though wanting to screw it up and
throw it away.

'Well, child, how are we going to answer that?'

'You know quite well, Madame.'

'Oh no, I don't. Times are hard, your family has suffered
financial losses, your sisters' affairs are in a bad state and
they both have large families. Your parents made crippling
sacrifices for them when they were married and are now
facing ruin to help them. It is impossible for them to estab-
lish you, they have worked out their budget on the supposition that you have taken the habit, and your action has
given rise to hopes. News that your final vows are imminent
has been noised abroad. Of course you can always count on
all my help. I have never tried to entice anybody into the
religious life; it is a state into which God calls us, and it is
very dangerous to bandy arguments with Him. I shall not
undertake to speak to your heart if the grace of God has no
message for it. So far I cannot lay the blame on myself for
the unhappiness of any other woman – would I wish to begin with you, my child, who are so dear to me? I am well
aware that you took the first steps because I persuaded you,
and I will not let that fact be abused in order to involve you
in anything you don't wish. So let us just think about it
together and come to a decision. Do you want to make your
vows?'

'No, Madame.'

'The religious life has no attraction for you?'

'No, Madame.'

'You won't obey your parents?'

'No, Madame.'

'Then what do you want to be?'

'Anything rather than a nun. I don't want to be a nun,
and I won't.'

'Very well, you won't. Well, now, we must think out an
answer to your mother.'

We agreed on a few ideas. She wrote the letter and
showed it to me, and once again I thought it was quite

good. But the director of the house was sent to me, likewise the theologian who had made the exhortation when I took the novice's habit, I was put into touch with the novice-mistress, I saw the Bishop of Aleppo, I had to argue with certain pious women who concerned themselves with my business without my knowing who they were. There were continual discussions with monks and priests, my father came, my sisters wrote and last of all my mother appeared. I resisted them all. Meanwhile the day for my final vows was fixed, no efforts were spared to obtain my consent, but when they realized it was useless to try to get it they decided to do without.

From that time on I was confined to my cell, silence was imposed on me, I was kept apart from everybody and left to myself; it was clear to me that they were resolved to settle my fate regardless of me. I was determined not to commit myself, that was quite definite, and all the real or false terrors they kept subjecting me to left me quite unshaken. But I was in a deplorable state, I didn't know how long it would go on, and if it came to an end I knew even less what might happen to me next. Amid all these uncertainties I came to a decision which you can judge as you please. I now saw nobody, neither Superior, novice-mistress nor my companions, so I sent a message to the first of these and pretended that I was coming round to my parents' wishes. But my plan was to put a dramatic end to this persecution by publicly protesting against the violence they were proposing to do me. So I said that they were the masters of my fate and could do as they pleased and settle it as they liked, that as they insisted I should make my profession I would do so. Thereupon the whole house gave itself up to rejoicing and the endearments came back with all manner of flattery and charm. God had spoken to my heart, nobody was better qualified for the state of perfection than I. It was impossible that it could be otherwise, they had always expected it. You could not fulfil your duties with such edifying constancy unless you had really had the call. The novice-mistress had never seen a more clearly marked vocation in any of her charges. She had been astonished at the curious caprice that had come over me, but she had always said to our Superior that they must hold on and it would pass, that the best nuns had moments like this, that they were suggestions of the Evil One who redoubled his efforts when he was on the point of losing his prey, that I was going to elude him, and henceforth it would be roses, roses all the way for me; that I should find the obligations of the religious life all the easier to bear because I had formed an exaggerated idea of them, that this sudden pressure on the yoke was a grace from Heaven which used this way of lightening it, and so on. It seemed not a little strange that the same thing could come from God or the devil according to the way they chose to look at it. There are many similar situations in religion, and my would-be comforters have often said of my thoughts either that they were so many suggestions of Satan or so many inspirations from God. The same evil comes either from God who is testing us or from Satan who is tempting.

I behaved with circumspection and felt I could look after myself. I saw my father who addressed me coolly, I saw my mother and she kissed me, I received letters of congratulation from my sisters and others. I learned that a Monsieur Sornin, parish priest of Saint-Roch, would preach the sermon and that a Monsieur Thierry, Chancellor of the University, would receive my vows. Everything went well until the eve of the great day, except that having heard that the ceremony was to be held in private, with very few people present, and that the doors of the church would be open only to relatives, I sent word by the gatekeeper to everybody in the neighbourhood, friends both male and female, and I got permission to write to some of my acquaintances. All this unexpected crowd of people appeared and had to be admitted, which produced the sort of assembly I wanted for my project. Oh Sir, what a night that preceding one was! I never got into the bed, but just sat on it. I called upon God to help me, I raised my hands to Heaven which I called upon to witness the violence being done to me. I visualized the part I was going to play before the altar, a girl protesting loudly against an act she seemed to have agreed to, the scandalized congregation, the despair of the nuns, the fury of my parents. 'Oh God, what is to become of me?' As I said these words a faintness came over me and I fell lifeless on my pillow. This fainting fit was followed by a shivering in which my knees knocked together and my teeth chattered, and then came a terrible fever and my mind wandered. I have no recollection either of undressing or leaving my cell, and yet I was found lying outside the Superior's door in nothing but my shift and almost lifeless. I learned these details later. In the morning I found myself back in my cell and round my bed were the Superior, the novice-mistress and what are called the assistants. I was well nigh prostrate; they asked me a few questions, but it was clear from my answers that I had no knowledge of what had happened, and they didn't tell me. They asked how I felt, if I still stood by my pious resolve and whether I felt in a fit state to bear the fatigues of the day. I said I did, and contrary to their expectations nothing was altered.

Everything had been made ready the day before. The bells were rung to inform the world that a woman was about to be condemned to misery. Once again my heart beat suffocatingly. They came to adorn me, as this day is a full-dress occasion. Now that I recall all these ceremonies I think there was something very solemn and touching about them for an innocent young girl not drawn in other directions. I was led to the chapel, Mass was celebrated and the good priest, who credited me with a resignation I certainly did not possess, preached a long sermon in which every single word was the opposite of the truth. It was really ridiculous, all he said about my happiness, the grace I had been vouchsafed, my courage, my zeal, my fervour and all the other fine sentiments he imagined I had. The contrast between his eulogy and the public demonstration I was about to make disconcerted me, I had moments of misgiving, but not for long, for it made me realize all the more that I lacked the qualities required to make a good nun. At last the terrible moment came. When I was to advance to the place where I had to pronounce my final vows my legs refused to carry me; two of my companions supported me under the arms, on one of which lay my head, and my feet dragged along. I don't know what was going on in the minds of the people present, but they were watching a dying victim being dragged to the altar, and on all sides could be heard sighs and sobs, though I am quite sure that those of my father and mother were not to be heard among them. Everybody was standing, and some young people were standing on chairs or clinging to the bars of the grille. A heavy silence fell when the man presiding over my profession said: 'Marie-Suzanne Simonin, do you promise to speak the truth?'

'I promise.'

'Are you here of your own accord and your own free will?'

I answered 'No,' but the nuns surrounding me answered 'Yes' on my behalf.

'Marie-Suzanne Simonin, do you promise God chastity, poverty and obedience?'

I hesitated a moment, the priest waited, and I answered: 'No, Sir.'

He began again:

'Marie-Suzanne Simonin, do you promise God chastity, poverty and obedience?'

I answered in a louder voice:

'No, Sir, no.'

He stopped and said 'My child, pull yourself together and listen.'

'Monsignor,' I said, 'you are asking whether I promise God chastity, poverty and obedience. I heard what you said and my answer is no.'

And turning round to face the people, among whom a loud murmur had arisen, I made a sign that I wished to speak. The murmur died down and I said:

'Gentlemen, and you especially, my own father and mother, I call you all to witness . . .'

At these words one of the sisters let the curtain fall over the grille and I realized it was useless to go on. The nuns crowded round and bitterly upbraided me. I listened in silence. I was taken back to my cell and locked in.

Alone and left to my thoughts, I began to find comfort to my soul, I went over what I had done and had no regrets. I realized that after the scandal I had caused it would be impossible for me to stay in this place for long, and perhaps they would not dare to send me to another convent. I didn't know what they would do with me, but I could think of nothing worse than to be a nun against one's will. There I remained for quite a time without having any news of anybody. Those who brought me food put my dinner down on the floor and went away without a word. After a month of this I was brought some ordinary clothing, I changed out of the habit, the Superior came and told me to follow her. I followed her to the main door of the convent, where I got into a carriage in which I found my mother waiting for me alone. I took the seat in front and the carriage set off. We sat opposite each other for some time without a word, my eyes were lowered and I dared not look at her. I don't know what went on in my innermost soul, but suddenly I flung myself at her feet and laid my head on her knees, saying nothing, but sobbing and gasping for breath. She pushed me away roughly. I did not get up, my nose began to bleed, I nevertheless seized one of her hands and made it wet with mingled tears and blood as I kissed it, saying: 'You are still my mother and I am still your child.' She pushed me even more roughly, snatched her hand away from mine and said: 'Get up, you miserable girl, get up.' I obeyed, sat back on the seat and drew my hood over my face. She had put such firm authority into her tone of voice that I felt I ought to spare her the very sight of me. My tears and the blood from my nose mingled together and ran down my arms, and I had it all over me before I noticed. I gathered from the few words she said that her dress and underclothes had been stained and that it annoyed her. We reached home and I was taken straight to a little room that had been made ready. On the way up the stairs I once again flung myself at her feet and held her by her dress, but the only result was that she turned round and looked at me, and there was such indignation in the set of her head, her mouth and her eyes that you can imagine it better than I can describe.

I entered my new prison, where I spent six months, begging in vain every day for the favour of speaking to her, of seeing my father or writing to them. My food was brought to me, I was looked after, a maid took me to Mass on Sundays and Holy-days of Obligation and brought me back to my solitary confinement. I read, did needlework, wept and sometimes sang, and thus the days passed. I was upheld by a secret conviction that I was free, and that my destiny, however hard it appeared, could change. But it was decided that I was to become a nun, and I did.

All this inhumanity and hardness of heart on my parents' part finally corroborated what I had suspected about my birth, and I have never found any other excuse for them. Apparently my mother was afraid that one day I should come back to the subject of the sharing of property and demand my legal share, thus associating a natural child with legitimate ones. But what had been only a supposition was to become a certainty.

While I was confined to the house I seldom performed any public religious duties. However, I was sent to confession on the eve of the major Holy Days. I have told you that I had the same confessor as my mother; I spoke to him and told him the whole story of the cruel way I had been treated for the past three years or so. He already knew it. I was especially bitter and resentful about my mother. This man, who had gone into the priesthood late in life, was a kindly soul, and he heard me out quietly and then said:

'My child, pity your mother, pity her more than blame her. She is good at heart, be assured that she is behaving like this in spite of herself.'

'In spite of herself, Sir? And who is there to force her? Did she not bring me into the world? What difference is there between my sisters and me?'

'A big difference.'

'A big one! I don't understand your answer at all.'

I was about to embark upon a comparison between my sisters and myself, but he stopped me and said:

'Now look, it is not inhumanity that is wrong with your parents. Try to bear your lot with patience and make a virtue of it in the eyes of God. I will see your mother, and you can be sure that any influence I may have upon her will be used on your behalf...'

This answer, *a big difference*, was a flash of illumination, and I was now sure of the truth of what I had suspected about my birth.

The following Saturday at about half past five in the afternoon, towards dusk, the maid who looked after me came up and said: 'Madame orders you to get dressed...' An hour later: 'Madame wishes you to come down with me.' A carriage was waiting at the door, and the maid and I got in. I was told that we were going to the Feuillants to see Father Séraphin. He was waiting for us alone. The maid went off and I entered the parlour and sat down with mingled foreboding and curiosity about what he was going to say. It was this:

'Mademoiselle, you are going to hear the explanation of your parents' harsh behaviour. I have had your mother's permission. You are sensible, you are intelligent and have reached an age when you could be trusted with a secret even if it didn't concern yourself. A long while ago I first urged your mother to reveal the secret you are about to learn, but she could never make up her mind to do so. It is hard for a mother to confess a grievous sin to her own child; you know what her character is, and it is scarcely of a kind to accept the sort of humiliation a certain admission brings. She thought she could guide you to what she planned without having to do this, but she was mistaken, and is mortified about it. So now she has come round to my advice and she herself has asked me to tell you that you are not Monsieur Simonin's child.'

'I suspected as much,' was my immediate answer.

'Now look, Mademoiselle, just weigh everything up and decide whether your mother, with or without your father's consent, can treat you in the same way as children whose sister you are not; whether she can confess to your father an offence about which he already has all too many suspicions.'

'But, Sir, who is my father?'

'That, Mademoiselle, I have not been told. But what is all too clear,' he went on, 'is that your sisters have been given an enormous advantage over you, and that every imaginable precaution has been taken, by marriage contracts, alienation of property, stipulations, trust funds and other means, to reduce your legal share to a minimum in case some day you are in a position to have recourse to the law to claim restitution. If you lose your parents you will find you have very little; you refuse to go to a convent now, but you may regret not being in one.'

'That is not possible, Sir. I am not asking for anything.'

'You don't know what hardship, toil and poverty mean.'

'At least I know the value of freedom and the burden of a state for which one has no vocation.'

'I have told you what I had to tell you; it is for you to give it due thought.'

He stood up.

'But just one more question, Sir.'

'Ask whatever you like.'

'Do my sisters know what you have told me?'

'No, Mademoiselle.'

'Then how have they been able knowingly to rob their own sister? For that is what they think I am.'

'Ah, Mademoiselle, self-interest, self-interest! They would never have been able to make the very advantageous marriages they have. In this world each is for himself, and I don't advise you to count on them if you happen to lose your parents. Be assured that they will dispute every penny of the little portion you will have to share with them. They have several children, and that is all too good an excuse for reducing you to beggary. And besides, there is nothing they can do; it is their husbands who control everything, and had they any feelings of sympathy, any assistance they gave unknown to their husbands would become a source of domestic dissension. I see that kind of thing all the time – abandoned children, or even illegitimate ones, helped at the cost of peace in the home. And then, Mademoiselle, charity bread is very bitter. If you take my advice you will make it up with your parents, do what your mother is bound to expect of you and enter the religious life. Then you will have a small allowance on which you will live, if not quite happily, at least reasonably so. Besides, I won't conceal the fact that your mother's repudiation of you and her determination to shut you away, as well as various other circumstances I cannot now recall, but which I have known about in the past, have had exactly the same effect on your father as on you. He had his suspicions about your birth, now he has none, and although he is not in the secret he is now quite sure that the only way you are his child is by virtue of the law which attributes children to the man who bears the name of husband. Come, Mademoiselle, you are good and sensible, reflect on what you have been told.'

I stood up, but burst into tears. I saw he was upset too. He slowly raised his eyes to Heaven and then saw me out again. I joined the maid who had come with me, we got back into the carriage and returned home.

It was late. Part of the night and the next day were spent in turning over in my mind what had been revealed to me. I had no father, religious scruples had deprived me of a mother, precautions had been taken against my claiming the rights of legitimate birth, there was nothing but harsh domestic captivity, no hope, no resource. Perhaps, had the situation been explained earlier, after my sisters' marriages, I might have been kept at home where there was no lack of visitors, and some man might have appeared who considered my character, intelligence, face and talents a sufficient dowry. That was still not quite impossible, but the sensation I had caused in the convent made it more difficult, for it is hardly credible that a girl of seventeen or eighteen could have gone to such lengths without uncommon strength of character. Men praise this quality highly, but it seems to me that they are glad to dispense with it in women they propose to take for their wives. Nevertheless it was a course of action to try before thinking of some other way, and I decided to take my mother into my confidence, and so asked for an interview, which was granted.

It was winter time. She was sitting in an armchair in front of the fire, she had a stern expression, stared straight in front of her and her features remained rigid. I went up to her, threw myself at her feet and begged forgiveness for all the wrong things I had done.

'That,' she answered, 'will depend on what you are going to say. Get up; your father is away and you have plenty of time to say what you want. You have seen Father Séraphin and at last you know what you are and what you can expect from me, unless your intention is to punish me all my life for a sin I have already more than paid for. Well, Mademoiselle, what do you want me to do? What have you decided?'

'Mother,' I answered, 'I know I possess nothing and can expect nothing. Far be it from me to wish to add to your troubles, whatever they may be, but you might have found me more willing to fit in with your wishes if you had acquainted me earlier with certain circumstances it was difficult for me to guess at. However, I know now, I know what I am, and it only remains for me to live as befits my state. I am no longer surprised at the distinctions that have been made between my sisters and myself, I see the justice of them and agree. But I am still your child, you have carried me in your womb, and I hope that you will not forget that.'

'I deserve all this misery,' she went on quickly, 'for not having told you as much as was in my power!'

'Well then, mother,' I said, 'give me back your love and physical presence, restore to me the affection of the man who thinks he is my father.'

'But he is almost as certain about the facts of your birth as you and I are. I never see you near him without being conscious of his reproaches, which he aims at me through the harshness of his treatment of you. You can never hope for any fatherly affection from him. And besides, I must confess, you are a constant reminder of such hateful betrayal and ingratitude on the part of another man that I cannot bear the thought; the vision of this man always rises up between you and me, he spurns me, and the loathing I have for him recoils upon you.'

'What!' I said, 'can't I even hope that you and Monsieur Simonin will treat me like an unknown child you took in out of charity?'

'We neither of us can. My child, don't poison my life any longer. If you had no sisters I know what my course of action should be, but you have two, and both have large families. The infatuation that gave me strength has been dead a long while now, and conscience has renewed its claims.'

'But the man responsible for my being brought into the world...'

'He is no more, he died without giving you a thought, and that is the least of his crimes.'

As she said this her expression hardened, her eyes began to blaze and her face was suffused with indignation; she wanted to say something but could not frame the words for the quivering of her lips. She was seated, and she buried her head in her hands to prevent my seeing the violent spasms shaking her. She remained in this condition for some time, then rose to her feet and walked round the room several times without uttering a word, holding back the tears that were forcing themselves out of her eyes. Then she said:

'The monster! For all he cared he might have murdered you in my body with all the sufferings he made me endure, but God preserved both you and me so that the mother might atone for her sin through her child. My dear girl, you possess nothing and never will. The little I am able to do for you is taken from your sisters, and all this is the outcome of one weak moment. But I hope I shall have nothing on my conscience when I die – I shall have paid for your dowry out of my savings. I don't take advantage of my husband's open-handedness, but I put aside day by day what he gives me now and again out of generosity. I have sold such jewels as I had, with his permission to spend the proceeds how I like. I used to like gambling, but I never do now; I used to love the theatre, but I have done without; I used to love society, and I live in retirement; I used to like display, but I have given it up. If you take the vow, which is my desire and Monsieur Simonin's, your dowry will be made up out of what I manage to put by each day.'

'But mother, there are still some well-to-do people coming here, and perhaps somebody will come who likes me for what I am and won't even want the savings you have earmarked for setting me up.'

'You must give up any such idea, the scandal you have created has disgraced you.'

'Is the evil beyond remedy?'

'Beyond remedy.'

'But must I be shut up in a convent just because I don't find a husband?'

'Unless you want to prolong my grief and remorse until my eyes are closed in death. For that must come, and at that terrible moment your sisters will be at my bedside – how can I see you with them, what effect would your presence have in these last moments? My daughter – for such you are whatever I do – your sisters have by law a name you only have because of a crime – don't torture your dying mother, let her go down in peace to her grave, let her be able to tell herself, when she is on the point of appearing before the Great Judge, that she has atoned for her sin as far as lay in her power, let her comfort herself with the thought that after her death you will not bring dissension into our home and will not claim rights that are not yours to claim.'

'Mother, set your mind at rest over that, summon a lawyer, let him draw up an act of renunciation, and I will sign anything you wish.'

'That cannot be done, a child cannot disinherit himself, that is the prerogative of parents who have reason to be angry. If it pleased God to take me tomorrow, then tomorrow I should be obliged to take the extreme step and tell my husband everything so that we could agree on the measures to be taken. Don't make me liable to commit an unwise act that would cause him to look upon me with hatred and necessarily bring dishonour upon you. If you survive me you will have no name, no money and no position. Tell me, wretched girl, what will become of you, what thoughts do you want me to carry away in death? Well, I shall have to tell your father ... But what can I say? That you aren't his daughter! My child, if it were only necessary to throw myself at your feet to make you ... But you have no feelings, you have your father's hardness of heart.'

At that moment Monsieur Simonin came in. He loved his wife, he saw the state she was in, he was a violent man. He stopped dead, gave me a terrible look and said:

'Leave this room!'

If he had been my real father I would not have obeyed him, but he was not.

Then he said to the servant who was carrying the light:

'Tell her never to show her face here again.'

I withdrew to my little prison. I thought over what my mother had said, I fell upon my knees and prayed God to show me what to do. I prayed a long time, I lay with my face to the floor. We seldom call upon the voice of God unless we don't know ourselves what to decide, and at such times He rarely advises us to do other than obey. That was the decision I reached. 'They want me to become a nun, perhaps it is also the will of God. Very well, so be it, since it is my fate to be unhappy what does it matter where?' I instructed the maid who served me to let me know when my father went out. The next day I asked for an interview with my mother, who sent me an answer that she had promised Monsieur Simonin not to see me, but that I could write to her with a pencil that was given me. So I wrote on a piece of paper (this fateful paper was preserved and it was used all too well against me):

'Mother, I am sorry for all the sorrows I have caused you, and I beg forgiveness and mean to end them. Order me to do whatever you wish, and if it is your desire that I should go into religion I trust it is God's also.'

The maid took the note to my mother, and came back a minute later, beaming with joy.

'Mademoiselle, as you only had one word to say to make your father and mother happy, as well as yourself, why did you wait so long before saying it? Monsieur and Madame look like I have never seen them do since I have been here. They were always bickering over you. Thank God I shan't see any more of that.'

While she was talking I felt as though I had just signed my own death warrant, and this presentiment will come true, Sir, if you desert me.

A few days went by without any news reaching me, and then one morning at nine my door opened suddenly; it was Monsieur Simonin, in his dressing gown and nightcap. Since I had known that he was not my father his presence had filled me with terror. I jumped up and curtseyed. At that moment I felt as though I had two hearts. I could not think of my mother without emotion and wanting to cry, but that was far from the case with Monsieur Simonin. What is certain is that a father inspires a kind of emotion one has for nobody else, but you don't appreciate this until you have found yourself, as I did, with a man who has fulfilled that august function for a long time and has just ceased to do so. And nobody else will ever understand what it means. If I went from his presence to my mother's I felt a different person. He said:

'Suzanne, do you recognize this letter?'

'Yes, Sir.'

'Did you write it of your own free will?'

'I can hardly say that.'

'But at any rate you are resolved to carry out what it undertakes?'

'I am.'

'Have you no preference for any particular convent?'

'No, they are all the same to me.'

'That will do.'

Those were my actual words, but unfortunately they were not written down. A fortnight went by during which I was totally ignorant of what was going on. I assumed that they had applied at various religious houses, and that the scandal of my earlier demonstration had prevented my being accepted as a postulant. At Longchamp they were less particular, and that was perhaps because it had been hinted to them that I was musical and had a good voice. A great deal was made of the trouble it had been and the great favour being done over my acceptance in that convent – I was even urged to write to the Mother Superior myself. I did not then realize the implications of this written testimony they required of me – apparently they were afraid that some day I might go back on my vows, and wanted to have a statement in my own hand that those vows had been freely taken. Unless that was the object how did it come about that that letter, which should have remained in the Mother Superior's possession, passed later into that of my brothers-in-law? But let us quickly close our eyes to that, for it shows Monsieur Simonin in a light I do not want to see. He is no more.

I was taken to Longchamp, and my mother came with me. I did not ask to say goodbye to Monsieur Simonin, and I confess I only thought of it when we were on the way. I was expected, the account of my adventures and of my talents had preceded me. Nothing was said about the former, but they were very anxious to see whether this new acquisition was worth it. When we had talked about many trivial matters, for after what had happened to me you can rest assured that no allusion was made to God, a vocation, the perils of the world, or the comforts of the religious life, and not a single word was risked of the pious platitudes with which these moments are generally filled, the Mother Superior said: 'Mademoiselle, you are musical, you sing, we have a harpsichord, and if you would care to go into the parlour ...' I felt sick at heart, but it was not the moment to show repugnance; my mother went through, I followed, and the Mother Superior brought up the rear with a few nuns who had come out of curiosity. It was evening, candles were brought in for me and I sat down at the instrument. I went on strumming for a long time, trying to find some piece out of my head, which is usually full of them, but not succeeding. But the Superior insisted, and so, with no ulterior motive, but simply by force of habit because I knew it so well, I sang *Tristes apprêts, pâles flambeaux, jour plus affreux que les ténèbres,** etc. I don't know what effect that produced, but they didn't listen for long; I was interrupted by praises which I was surprised to have earned so quickly and with so little effort. My mother handed me over to the Superior, gave me her hand to kiss and took herself off.

So there I was in another religious house, as a postulant and with every appearance of being so of my own free will. But you, Sir, who know everything that has happened as far as this point, what do you think? Most of these things were not brought up when I wanted to renounce my vows, some because they were true but impossible to prove, others because they would have made me look odious without helping me in any way – I would simply have looked like an unnatural child vilifying the memory of her parents in order to obtain her freedom. There were proofs of what was *against* me, but what was *for* me could not be brought up or proved. I would not even let them give the judge any hint about my birth; some people who knew nothing about the law advised me to call in my mother's and father's confessor, but that could not be done, and even if it had been possible I would not have entertained the idea. Oh, and by the way, in case I forget and your desire to help me prevents your thinking of it, I think, subject to your superior

* An aria from Rameau's opera *Castor et Pollux* (1737). – Trans.

judgement, we ought to keep quiet about my being musical and able to play, for that would in itself be enough to betray my identity, and the display of these talents doesn't fit in with the obscurity and security I long for. People in my walk of life do not possess this knowledge, and I had better not. If I am forced to go abroad I will utilize it. Go abroad! Tell me why this idea fills me with horror. I don't know where I should go. I am young and inexperienced, I am afraid of poverty, men and vice. I have always lived a sheltered life, and if I were away from Paris I should think I was adrift in the wide world. None of that may be true, but that is how I feel. Sir, I don't know where to go or what is to become of me, it all depends on you.

At Longchamp, as at most religious houses, the Mother Superior is changed every three years. When I was taken there a certain Madame de Moni was beginning her term of office. I cannot speak too highly of her, and yet it was her goodness that was my undoing. She was a sensible woman who understood the human heart, she was indulgent, though nobody needed to exercise it less, for we were all her children. She only ever noticed misdeeds she could not help seeing, or the gravity of which would not let her close her eyes to them. In saying this I have no axe to grind; I did my duty meticulously, and she would be just enough to agree that I did nothing that she had either to punish or overlook. If she made any distinction it was based on merit, and that being said I don't know whether I ought to tell you that she had a great affection for me and that I was by no means the least of her favourites. I know that this is very great self-praise, and greater than you can imagine, since you did not know her. The word favourite is that used by the others out of envy for the ones the Mother Superior loves. If there were anything I could find fault with in Madame de Moni it would be that she let her taste for virtue, piety, candour, meekness, talent and integrity be seen too obviously and that she was not unaware of the resulting humiliation of those who could not claim these qualities. She also had a gift, perhaps more frequent in the convent than in the world, of quickly summing up people's characters. It was unusual for a nun who did not please her at the outset ever to please her afterwards. She soon approved of me, and from the beginning I had the utmost confidence in her. They were unfortunate indeed whose confidence she had difficulty in winning! They must be bad, irretrievably bad, and know it. She raised the subject of my adventure at Sainte-Marie, and I told her the story with no reservations just as I have told you – I told her everything I have written to you, everything to do with my birth and troubles, nothing was forgotten. She pitied and consoled me, and led me to hope for a happier future.

And so the period of my postulancy came to an end and the time came for taking the habit, and I took it. I went through my novitiate without any feeling of distaste, and I pass quickly over these two years because there was nothing unhappy about them except a feeling inside me that I was moving step by step towards entering a calling for which I was not suited. Sometimes this feeling came over me very strongly, but then I would go straight to my good Mother Superior who embraced me, strengthened my purpose, reasoned powerfully with me and always ended by saying: 'And don't other walks in life have their thorns also? We only feel our own. Come along, my child, let us kneel down and pray ...'

She would then prostrate herself and pray aloud, but with such sweetness and eloquence, gentleness, exaltation and strength that you would have said she was inspired by the spirit of God. Her thoughts, expressions and parables went straight to your very heart. At first you listened, then little by little you were borne along, you were one with her, your soul thrilled and you shared her ecstasy. Yet her object was not seduction, but that is what she achieved, for when you left her your heart was on fire, joy and ecstasy shone on your face, and your tears were so sweet! It was an impress that came upon her and remained a long time with her, and we kept it too. For I am not basing this on my experience alone, but that of all the nuns. Some of them have told me that they felt a longing for consolation spring up within them like the desire for a great pleasure, and I think I might have reached that state myself had I grown more accustomed to the experience.

And yet, as the time for my profession drew near, I fell into such a deep depression that it put my dear Mother Superior to the severest test. Her skill abandoned her, as she herself admitted to me. 'I don't know,' she said, 'what is happening to me. It seems that when you come to me, God withdraws and my spirit falls silent, and in vain I try to work myself up, I hunt for ideas and seek to lift up my heart. I find I am just an ordinary woman and an insignificant one, and I am afraid to say anything...' 'Ah, dear Mother,' I said, 'what a presentiment! Suppose it were God making you silent!'

One day when I was more perplexed and downcast than ever, I went to her cell. At first the sight of me filled her with confusion, for clearly she could read in my eyes and in my whole person that the deep emotion within me was beyond her power to touch, and she was loth to struggle without the certainty of winning. But she did make the attempt, and gradually she warmed to the task, and as my depression waned so her enthusiasm waxed – she suddenly fell upon her knees and I did the same. I believed I was about to share her ecstasy, and wanted to, but she said a few words and then suddenly stopped. I waited in vain, she said no more but rose to her feet, burst into tears, took my hand and held me in her arms. 'Ah, my dear child,' she said, 'what a cruel effect you have had upon me! Well, it's no use going on, I can feel that the spirit has gone out of me. So may God speak to you Himself, since it does not please Him to do so through my mouth.'

And it was true. I don't know what had been happening inside her, whether I had filled her with misgivings about her own strength which never left her again, whether I had made her self-conscious, or whether I had really broken her communication with God, but she never regained her gift of consolation. On the eve of my profession I went to see

her, and her melancholy was equal to mine. I began to weep
and so did she, I threw myself at her feet, she blessed me,
raised me to my feet again and sent me away saying: 'I am
weary of life and long for death. I have asked God not to let
me see this day, but it is not His will. Well, I shall speak to
your mother, I shall spend the night in prayer and you
must pray too. But go to bed, I insist.'

'Let me pray with you.'

'I will let you from nine until eleven, but no longer. At
nine-thirty I shall begin to pray, and so will you, but at
eleven you will leave me to pray alone, and you will rest.
There, my dear child, I will spend the whole night before
God.'

She tried to pray, but could not. I slept, but the saintly
woman went along the corridors knocking at each door,
waking the nuns and making them go noiselessly down into
the church. They all went there and when everybody was
assembled she invited them to intercede for me. At first this
prayer was made in silence, then she put out the lights and
together they all recited the *Miserere*, except the Mother
Superior, who was prostrate before the altar, mortifying
herself cruelly, saying: 'Oh God, if it is because of some sin
I have committed that you have forsaken me, grant me
forgiveness. I do not ask that you should restore the gift
you have taken from me, but that you yourself speak to this
innocent girl now asleep while I am pleading here for her.
Lord, speak to her, speak to her parents and forgive me.'

Early the next morning she came to my cell; I didn't hear
her for I was not yet awake. She sat at my bedside, laid one
hand gently on my forehead and looked at me with anxiety,
bewilderment and grief passing in succession across her face,
and that is how she appeared to me when I opened my eyes.
She made no mention of what had been happening during
the night, but only asked me if I had gone to bed early, and
I answered:

'At the time you told me to.'

Had I slept well?

'Deeply.'

'I expected you would.' And how was I feeling?

'Very well. And you, Reverend Mother?'

'Alas, I have never seen anybody enter the religious life without feeling anxiety for them, but never with any one of them have I felt so much worry as over you. I do so much want you to be happy.'

'If you always love me, I shall be.'

'Ah, if it only depended on that! Didn't you think of anything during the night?'

'No.'

'No dreams?'

'No.'

'What is going on now in your heart?'

'I am dazed, I am fulfilling my destiny without finding it repugnant or attractive, I feel I am being carried along by necessity and am letting myself go. Oh, Reverend Mother, I feel none of that sweet joy, thrill, melancholy or pleasurable anxiety I have sometimes observed in others when they were at the stage I am now. I am numb, I cannot even cry. It is insisted on, it has to be done, and that is the only thought I have about it. But you are not saying anything.'

'I have not come to talk to you, but to see you and listen to what you have to say. I am expecting your mother, try not to upset me, but let my emotions build up within me, and when I can contain no more I will leave you. I must stay quiet. I know myself, and I act on the first impulse, but it is violent and I don't want it to work itself off on you. Just rest a little longer and let me look at you, just say a few words and let me find here what I have come to look for. I will go away and God will do the rest...'

I fell silent, lay back on my pillow and held out one hand to her, which she took. She seemed to be meditating, and meditating deeply. She kept her eyes tightly shut, but now and again opened them, looked heavenwards and then back at me; she became agitated, her soul was troubled, recovered its calm and then grew troubled again. Truly this woman was born to be a prophetess, she had both the face and the character. She had once been beautiful, but age,

while making her features sag, had nevertheless added
more dignity to her face by stamping deep lines on it. Her
eyes were small, but they seemed either to be looking into
herself or right through nearby things so as to read beyond,
far away into the past or future. Sometimes she gripped my
hand tightly. Then she suddenly asked me the time.

'Nearly six.'

'Good-bye, I am going. They are coming to dress you, and
I don't want to be here, for it would distract my attention. I
have only one thing to worry about, and that is to observe
moderation for the first few minutes.'

She had hardly gone out before the novice-mistress and
my fellows entered; my religious habit was taken off and I
was dressed in secular clothes – you know the custom. I
heard nothing of what was being said round me, I had
almost reached the state of an automaton. I saw nothing,
but occasionally little convulsive shudders ran over me. I
was told what to do, and often it had to be repeated because
I did not understand the first time, and I did it. It was not
that I was thinking of anything else, but I was absorbed,
and my head was weary as though exhausted after hard
thinking. While all this was going on the Mother Superior
was in conversation with my mother. I never knew what
happened during this interview, which went on a long time,
but I was told that when they separated my mother was so
upset that she could not find the door she had come in by,
and that the Mother Superior had emerged pressing
clenched fists to her forehead.

However, the bells rang and I went down. There were
only a few people present. The sermon may have been good
or bad, I didn't hear. I was merely a puppet all through that
morning, which was non-existent in my life, for I never
knew how long it lasted, what I did or what I said. Presumably I was questioned, presumably I replied. I pronounced vows, but I have no recollection of them, and I
found I had become a nun as passively as I was made a
Christian, for I understood no more about the ceremony of
my profession than about my baptism; with this difference,

that the one confers grace and the other presupposes it. Well then, Sir, although I didn't protest at Longchamp as I had done at Sainte-Marie, do you consider me any the more bound? I appeal to your judgement as I appeal to the judgement of God. I was in such a state of collapse that when some days later I was told that I was to be in the choir, I didn't know what they meant. I asked if it was really true that I had made my profession. I wanted to see the signature with my own eyes, and the witness of the whole community and of the few outsiders who had been asked to the ceremony had to be added to these proofs. Several times I said to the Mother Superior: 'Is it really true?' and always expected her to answer: 'No, my child, you are being deceived.' Her repeated assurances did not convince me, for I could not believe that out of a whole day, and one so stormy and full of strange and unusual events, I could not remember one single thing, not even the faces of those who had supported me nor that of the priest who had preached, nor of the one who had accepted my vows. The only thing I can remember is changing from my religious habit into secular dress; from that moment on I was what you would call physically absent. It took me months on end to get out of that condition, and I attribute my profound ignorance of what happened to the length of this convalescence, as you might call it, like people who have been through a long illness, talked reasonably and received the last sacraments, and then, restored to health, have no recollection of it. I have seen several examples of this in the convent and have said to myself: 'I suppose that is what happened to me on the day I made my profession.' But it remains to be seen whether such things come from the person himself, and whether one is really involved, as one appears to be.

During that same year I lost three important figures in my life: my father, or rather the man who passed for my father, who was old, had worked hard and just faded away; then my Mother Superior and my own mother.

This admirable nun felt for a long time that her hour was approaching. She condemned herself to silence and had her coffin brought into her room. Sleep had gone from her and she spent whole days and nights meditating and writing; she left behind fifteen meditations which seem to me of the greatest beauty and I have a copy of them. If some day you are desirous of seeing the thoughts suggested by this moment of her existence, I would let you have them. They are entitled *The Last Moments of Sister de Moni.*

As her death was drawing near she had herself dressed. She was lying on her bed and received the last sacraments, holding a crucifix in her arms. It was night-time, and torches lit up the mournful scene. We were round her, all weeping, and the cell echoing with our lamentations, when suddenly a light came into her eyes and she sat up and spoke in a voice almost as strong as when she was in full health. Her lost gift came back and she reproached us for our tears, which seemed to begrudge her eternal bliss. 'My children, don't be deceived by your grief. It is there,' she went on, pointing upwards, 'it is there that I shall be helping you, my eyes will be constantly looking down upon this house. I shall intercede for you, and my intercession will be heard. Draw near, all of you, and let me kiss you, come and receive my blessing and farewell...' As she said these last words this unique woman passed away, leaving behind never-ending regrets.

My mother died late that autumn, on her return from a short visit she had paid to one of her daughters. There was some worry on her mind, and her health had already been very impaired. I never knew the name of my father or the circumstances of my birth. The priest who had been her confessor and mine handed me a little package on her behalf; it contained fifty louis and a letter, sewn up in a piece of cloth. This is what was in the letter:

'My child, this is not very much, but my conscience prevents my giving away a larger sum. This is what remains of what I have managed to save out of little gifts from Monsieur Simonin. Live a devout life, it is the best way for your happiness even in this world. Pray for me; your birth is the one serious sin I have committed. Help me to expiate it, and in consideration for the good works you will do may God forgive me for having brought you into this world. Above all do not upset the peace of the family, and although the choice of the state you have embraced has not been as whole-hearted as I might have wished, beware of changing it. Why was I not shut in a convent all my life? I would not now be so anguished by the thought that in a moment I must face the terrible judgement. Reflect, my child, that your mother's destiny in the other world depends largely upon your behaviour in this one. God, who sees all, will in His justice mete out to me all the good and all the evil you do. Farewell, Suzanne, ask nothing of your sisters, they are not in a position to help you; hope for nothing from your father, he has preceded me, he has seen the full light and he is waiting for me, but my presence will be less terrible for him than his for me. Farewell once again. Oh, wretched mother and unhappy child! Your sisters have come, and I am not pleased with them; they are taking things, carrying things away, and in front of a dying mother indulge in greedy quarrels which are torturing me. When they come near my bed I turn away, for what would I see? Two creatures in whom lack of money has killed all natural feeling. They are longing for the little I am leaving, they ask the doctor and nurse disgraceful questions which show the impatience with which they are waiting for the moment I go, which will put them in possession of everything surrounding me. They have had suspicions, I don't know how, that I might have some money hidden between my mattresses, and there is nothing they have not had recourse to in order to make me get out of bed. And they succeeded, but fortunately the person to whom I am entrusting this money had come the day before, and I had given him this little package, with this letter which he has written to my dictation. Burn this letter, and when you hear that I am no more, which will be soon now, have a Mass said for me and at it renew your vows, for I want you to remain in the religious life. The vision of you in the world with no help and support and so young, would be the final torment of my last moments.'

My father died on the 5th of January, my Mother Superior at the end of the same month and my mother the following Christmas.

Mother de Moni was succeeded by Sister Sainte-Christine. Oh Sir, what a difference between the one and the other! I have told you the sort of woman the first was. The latter had a petty character, her mind was narrow and filled with superstitions, she went in for modern ideas and had discussions with Sulpicians and Jesuits. She took a dislike to all the favourites of her predecessor, and in a moment the house was full of dissensions, hatred, back-biting, accusations, calumnies and persecutions. We had to argue about questions of theology we didn't understand in the least, subscribe to formulas, get used to strange practices. Mother de Moni disapproved of mortifying the flesh, and she had only scourged her own body twice in her life, once on the eve of my profession and once on a similar occasion. She said of such penances that they did not correct anyone of any failing but only served to fill people with pride. She wanted her nuns to be healthy, to have wholesome bodies and serene minds. The first thing she did when she found herself in charge was to have all hair-shirts and disciplines brought to her and forbid the spoiling of food with ashes, sleeping on the hard ground or obtaining any of these instruments. The new Superior, on the contrary, returned to each nun her hair-shirt and discipline, but had her Old and New Testaments taken away. The favourites of the previous reign are never the ones of the next. I signified nothing, to put it no worse than that, to the present Superior for the very reason that the previous one had liked me, but I hastened to make my position worse by actions you will call imprudent or steadfast according to the way you look at them.

The first thing I did was to give myself up to all the grief

I felt at the loss of our first Superior, and sing her praises on every occasion, make comparisons between her and our present ruler which were unfortunate for the latter, describe the state of the convent in previous years, call back to mind the peace we used to enjoy, the kindly treatment we had, the food, both spiritual and material, we used to be given, and laud to the skies the way of life, sentiments and character of Sister de Moni. The next was to throw my hairshirt into the fire and take off my discipline, preach on the subject to my friends and urge some of them to follow my example. The third was to provide myself with an Old and New Testament, and the fourth to dissociate myself from any sect and merely call myself a Christian, refusing to accept names like Jansenist or Molinist, the fifth to keep rigorously to the rule of the house and do nothing beyond it or short of it, and consequently not lend myself to any non-obligatory practices, for the obligatory ones seemed too rigorous as it was. For instance, I did not go into the organ loft except on Holy-days of Obligation, nor sing except when I was on choir duty, and put an end to letting them take advantage of my goodwill and my talents to make me do everything every day. I read and re-read our regulations and knew them by heart, so that if I was directed to do anything which was either not clearly set out therein or not there at all, or which seemed to contradict them, I refused absolutely, but took up the book and said: 'Here are the promises I made, and I made no others.'

My talk attracted a few followers. The authority of the mistresses was thus very curtailed, and they had to stop using us as slaves. Hardly a day went by without some scene. In cases of doubt my companions consulted me, and I was always on the side of the rules and against despotism. So I soon looked like a trouble-maker. The Archbishop's auxiliaries were constantly being appealed to. I appeared before them, defended myself and my companions, and not a single time was I found guilty, so careful was I to have right on my side. It was impossible to attack me on the question of my duties, which were scrupulously fulfilled. As to the little favours a Superior is always free to give or to withhold, I did not ask for any. I never appeared in the parlour, and as I knew nobody I had no visitors. But I had burned my hair-shirt and thrown away my discipline and urged others to do the same, neither would I listen to any discussion about Jansenism or Molinism one way or the other. When I was asked whether I submitted to the Constitution I answered that I did to the Church; asked whether I accepted the Bull I said that I accepted the Gospels. My cell was searched and they found the Old and New Testaments. I had let some indiscreet remarks escape me on the subject of the suspicious intimacy between some of the favourites; moreover the Superior went in for long and frequent interviews with a young priest, and I had discovered the reason and the pretext for these. I omitted none of the things needed to make myself feared and hated and to bring about my ruin, and in this I succeeded. They gave up complaining about me to higher authorities, and instead concentrated on making my life hard. The other nuns were forbidden to come near me and soon I was quite isolated. I had a few friends, and it was suspected that they would try to circumvent the ban imposed on them by visiting me at night or during forbidden hours, since they could not speak to me in the daytime. We were spied on, I was discovered with one or another, and they made the most of this imprudence by punishing me in the most inhuman manner. I was condemned to stay on my knees throughout the services for weeks on end, separated from the others in the centre of the choir, to live on bread and water, to remain shut in my cell and perform the most degrading domestic tasks. And my so-called accomplices were treated almost as badly. When nothing wrong could be found in my conduct, something was invented: I was given incompatible orders and punished for not having carried out both, the hours of meals and services were made earlier and without my being told the whole timetable of the convent was altered, so that in spite of the greatest care in the world I was in the wrong every day and every day punished. I have plenty of courage, but no courage in the world can hold out in the face of neglect, solitude and persecution. Things reached the stage when it became a game to torment me, the entertainment of fifty people in league. I cannot begin going into all the tiny details of these spiteful tricks. I was prevented from sleeping, from staying up, from praying. One day parts of my clothing were stolen, another time it was my keys or my breviary; the lock on my door was put out of order. Either I was prevented from doing something properly or what I had done properly was spoilt. Words and acts were attributed to me, I was made responsible for everything and my life was a sequence of real or imagined misdemeanours and their punishments.

My health did not stand up to such prolonged and hard ordeals, and I was overcome by exhaustion, grief and melancholy. In early days I sought strength and patience at the altar, and sometimes found it. I floated between resignation and despair, sometimes submitting to all the harshness of my lot, sometimes thinking of freeing myself by violent means. There was a deep well at the bottom of the garden – how many times did I go to it and look down into its depths! There was a stone bench beside it – how many times did I sit there with my head on the edge of the well! How many times, in the tumult of my mind, did I suddenly jump up, resolved to put an end to all my troubles! What held me back? Why did I prefer to weep, cry aloud, trample my veil underfoot, tear my hair and scratch my face with my nails? If it was God who stopped my destroying myself, why did He not prevent all these other occurrences too?

I am going to tell you something which may seem very strange to you, but is nevertheless true; it is that I have no doubt whatever that my frequent visits to the well were noticed, and that my cruel enemies hoped that one day I would carry out the scheme maturing in my heart. Whenever I moved in that direction they made a point of going the other way and of looking elsewhere. Several times I found the garden gate left open at hours when it should have been shut, and significantly on days when troubles had been heaped upon me. They had strained my violent character to breaking point, and thought my mind was deranged. But as soon as I thought I had realized that this way of quitting life was, so to speak, being offered to my despair, that I was being led by the hand to that well which I should always find ready to welcome me, I ceased to bother about it and my thoughts turned into other channels. I stood about in corridors and gauged the height of windows. At night, as I undressed, I unconsciously tested the strength of my garters. Another day I refused to eat; I went down to the refectory and stood with my back to the wall, hands dangling at my sides and eyes shut, refusing to touch any of the food they had set before me, but standing there in such a rapt state that I was still there when all the nuns had left. So a point was made of stealing off noiselessly and leaving me there, and then I was punished for having failed to be present at office. In fact, they turned me against almost every way of taking my own life because I felt that far from being discouraging they were making opportunities for me. Apparently we don't like being pushed out of this world, and perhaps I should not have still been here had they shown signs of wanting to keep me. When we take our own lives, perhaps it is to infuriate other people, and we might stay alive if we thought we were giving them satisfaction – these are very subtle processes going on within us. As a matter of fact, if I can recall the state I was in when I was by the well, it seems to me that deep within me I was crying out to these creatures who were moving away so as to facilitate a crime: 'Just take one step in my direction, show the slightest desire to save me, run to stop me, and rest assured that you will get here too late.' In fact I only went on living because they were wishing for my death. The urge to hurt and torment gradually wanes in the world outside; it never does in the cloister.

Things had reached that state when, thinking over my past life, the idea occurred to me of having my vows annulled. At first it was just a vague notion. Alone, abandoned, without support, how could I succeed in a project so full of difficulty even had I had that support? And yet this idea steadied me and my mind grew more collected, I was more myself, and I avoided troubles and bore more patiently those that came my way. This change in me was noticed and caused surprise, the spitefulness suddenly stopped, like a cowardly enemy who is pursuing you and whom you turn and face just when he is not expecting it. There is a question I would like to raise with you, Sir, and that is why, amidst all the wild ideas that pass through the mind of a nun driven to desperation, that of setting fire to the convent does not occur to her. I never had it, nor have others, although it is the easiest thing in the world to carry out. All you have to do is to take a torch on a windy day to a loft, a wood-pile or a corridor. There are no burnt convents, yet at such a time all doors are opened and free to all. Could it be that we fear a peril for ourselves and those we love, but scorn a way of escape which is common to us and to those we hate? This thought may be too subtle to be true.

By dint of thinking a thing over you feel its rightness and even its feasibility, and that gives you a position of strength. It took me a fortnight, for my mind works quickly. What did it involve? Drawing up a memorandum and getting it studied, and neither of these things was without danger. Since a revolution had come about in my mind, I was watched more attentively than ever, they followed me with their eyes, and I never took a step that was not investigated, never said a word that was not weighed. They made friendly overtures and tried to sound me, I was questioned, they simulated sympathy and friendship, they went back over my past life and only partially blamed me or even excused me, they hoped things would now improve, prospects of a happier future were held out. But they entered my cell at any moment, day or night, on any pretext. Suddenly, stealthily they would open my curtains and then go away. I had got into a habit of sleeping fully dressed, and I had developed another, which was writing out my regular confession. On those fixed days I went to the Superior and

asked for ink and paper, which she did not refuse. So now I
waited for confession day, and while waiting I mentally
composed what I had to do, which was an abridged version
of all I have written to you, but using false names. However, I did three stupid things: the first was to tell the
Superior that I should have a great deal to write, and therefore I asked for more paper than the usual allowance; the
second was to get on with my memorandum and do nothing about the confession; the third was that not having
written out my confession and being unprepared for this
religious observance, I only stayed a moment in the confessional. All this was noted, and the conclusion drawn that
the paper I had asked for had been used for some purpose
other than I had said. But if it had not been used for my
confession, as clearly it had not, to what use had I put
it?

Although I did not know that they would be so concerned about it, I felt that a document of this importance
must not be found in my possession. At first I thought of
sewing it inside my bolster or mattresses, then of concealing
it in my clothing, burying it in the garden, throwing it into
the fire. You would never believe what a hurry I was in to
get it written and how worried I was when it was written.
First I sealed it and hid it in my bosom, then went to
church, for the bell was ringing. My nervous state was be-
trayed by my movements. I sat next to a young nun who
was fond of me; sometimes I had seen her looking at me
with compassion and tears in her eyes. She did not speak to
me but certainly was distressed. Risking anything that
might happen to me I resolved to entrust my document to
her, so at the moment in the service when all nuns kneel,
bow their heads and are, so to speak, buried in their stalls, I
stealthily drew the paper from my bosom and held it out to
her behind me. She took it and thrust it into her own
bosom. This was the most important of the things she did for
me, but I had had many others done, for she had for
months past, without compromising herself, been busy re-
moving all the little obstacles they put in the way of per-

forming my duties so as to be able to punish me. She would come and knock at my door when it was time to come out, she would tidy up what had been deliberately upset, she went and rang the bell or answered when it was necessary, she was present wherever I was supposed to be; but I knew nothing about all this.

I was well advised to do what I did. As we left the choir the Superior said to me: 'Sister Suzanne, come with me.' I followed her, and then, stopping in the corridor at another door, she said: 'This is your cell. Sister Saint-Jerome will occupy yours.' I went in and so did she. We were both sitting there in silence when a nun appeared with clothes which she put down on a chair, and the Superior said to me: 'Sister Suzanne, take your clothes off and put on these.' I obeyed in front of her, while she watched my every movement. The sister who had brought the clothes was at the door; she came in, took away those I had discarded and disappeared, followed by the Superior. I was not told the reason for this behaviour, and I did not ask. But meanwhile they had searched everywhere in my cell, unsewn the pillow and mattresses, moved everything that could be moved or could have been moved, they had been step by step wherever I had been, to the confessional, the church, into the garden, to the well, to the stone bench. I saw some of this search going on and I guessed the rest. Nothing was found, but they were nevertheless convinced that there was something. They continued to spy on me for several days, going wherever I had been, looking everywhere, but in vain. At length the Superior thought that there was no possible way of finding out the truth except from me. So one day she came into my cell and said:

'Sister Suzanne, you have your faults, but lying is not one of them, so tell me the truth. What have you done with all the paper I gave you?'

'Reverend Mother, I have told you.'

'That cannot be true, because you asked for a lot and you were only a moment in the confessional.'

'That is so.'

'Then what have you done with it?'

'What I told you.'

'Very well, swear to me, on the holy obedience you have vowed to God, that that is so, and in spite of appearances I will believe you.'

'Reverend Mother, you have no right to put me on oath for such a trivial matter, and I am not allowed to swear either. I cannot do so.'

'You are deceiving me, Sister Suzanne, and you don't know what you are laying yourself open to. What have you done with that paper I gave you?'

'I have told you.'

'Where is it?'

'I haven't got it now.'

'What have you done with it?'

'What one usually does with such scribbles which are useless after they have served their purpose.'

'Swear to me, on holy obedience, that all of it was used for writing out your confession, and that you have none left.'

'Reverend Mother, I repeat, the second thing being no more important than the first, I cannot swear.'

'Swear,' she said, 'or else ...'

'I will not swear.'

'You will not?'

'No, Reverend Mother.'

'You are guilty, then?'

'What can I be guilty of?'

'Everything. There is nothing you are not capable of. You have gone out of your way to sing the praises of my predecessor so as to belittle me, to pour scorn on practices she abolished or regulations she abrogated and which I have felt it my duty to re-establish, to stir up the whole community, to infringe the regulations and set people against each other. You have made a point of failing to carry out your duties and forcing me to punish you and those you have influenced, which hurts me most of all. I could have acted in the harshest way towards you, but I

have been lenient; I believed that you would come to acknowledge your misdeeds, return to the spirit of your calling
and back to me, but you have not done so. Something is
going on in your soul which is evil, you are nursing some
project, and the interests of our house demand that I
should know what it is, and know it I will, you can rely on
that. Sister Suzanne, tell me the truth.'

'I have told you.'

'I am going out now, beware of my return ... No, I will
sit down and give you one more moment to make up your
mind ... Your papers, if they exist –'

'They don't exist now.'

'– or an oath that there was nothing in them except your
confession.'

'I cannot do that.'

She paused a moment in silence, then went out and came
back with four of her favourites who looked wild-eyed and
demented. I threw myself at their feet and implored their
pity. They shouted in chorus: 'No pity, Reverend Mother,
don't let your heart be touched, let her hand over her documents or be sent to the punishment cell.'* I clasped the
knees of each in turn, addressing them by name: 'Sister
Sainte-Agnes, Sister Sainte-Julie, what harm have I done to
you? Why are you turning Reverend Mother against me?
Have I ever behaved in that way? How many times have I
interceded for you? You have forgotten now. You were to
blame then, but now I am not.'

The Superior stood there motionless and said to me:

'Give up your documents, you wretched creature, or tell
us what was in them.'

'Reverend Mother,' they said, 'don't ask her for them any
more, you are too kind; you don't know what she is. She is
an intractable soul and can only be tamed by violent means.

* *qu'elle aille en paix*. Translated here as 'sent to the punishment cell', because it is a pun on the Latin *in pace*, which was
used as a euphemism for the horrible cell in which offenders
served their solitary confinement. Hence the reference, on page
81, to their sinister meaning of *Requiescat in pace*. – Trans.

Since she is forcing you to do this, so much the worse for her.'

'Dear Reverend Mother,' I said, 'I have done nothing to offend God or man, I swear to you.'

'That is not the oath I want.'

'She must have written some memorandum to the Vicar-General or the Archbishop against us, against you. God knows what picture she will paint of what goes on inside the convent, and people are eager to believe the worst. Madame, you must eliminate this creature unless you mean her to eliminate us.'

The Superior added: 'So you see, Sister Suzanne...'

I jumped up and said: 'Yes, Madame, I see everything, and I realize that I am destroying myself, but a moment sooner or a moment later is not worth bothering about. Do what you like with me, give in to their hatred, go through with your injustice.'

And I held out my arms to them. Her friends seized them. They tore off my veil and shamelessly stripped me. On my breast they found a miniature of our former Superior, which they took away. I begged them to let me kiss it once more, but they refused. They threw a shift at me, took off my stockings, covered me with a sack and took me along the passage bareheaded and barefoot. I screamed for help, but they had rung the bell to warn everybody to stay out of sight. I called on Heaven, I fell to the ground but they dragged me along. By the time I reached the bottom of the stairs my feet were bleeding and my legs bruised – my condition would have touched hearts of bronze. However, they unlocked with huge keys the door of a little dark underground cell and threw me on to some matting half rotten with damp. There I found a piece of black bread and a pitcher of water, with a few other necessary vessels of the coarsest kind. For a pillow you had to roll up one end of the mat, and on a stone block was a skull with a wooden crucifix. My first instinct was to put an end to myself; I tried to throttle myself, I tore my clothes with my teeth, uttering fearful cries and howling like a wild animal. I banged my head against the wall until I was covered with blood. In fact I went on trying to kill myself until my strength failed, which was not very long. There I stayed for three days; I thought it was going to be for the whole of my life. Each morning one of my torturers came and said:

'Obey Reverend Mother and you will get out of here.'

'I have done nothing wrong and don't know what is required of me. Oh, Sister Saint-Clement, if there is a God ...'

On the third day, at about nine in the evening, the door was opened. It was the same nuns who had taken me there. After singing the praises of our Superior they told me she was pardoning me and I was going to be set free.

'It is too late,' I said. 'Leave me here to die.'

But they lifted me up and dragged me back to my own cell, where I found the Superior.

'I have communed with God about your future, and He has touched my heart. His will is that I have pity on you, and I am obeying Him. Kneel down and ask for His forgiveness.'

I knelt down and said:

'Oh God, I pray for pardon for my misdeeds, even as You did for me on the Cross.'

'What pride!' they exclaimed. 'She compares herself with Jesus Christ and us with the Jews who crucified Him.'

'Do not look at me,' I said, 'but look at yourselves and judge.'

'That is not all,' went on the Superior. 'Swear to me, on holy obedience, that you will never say anything about what has happened.'

'Then what you have done must be very wrong, since you demand my oath to keep silence. Nobody will ever know anything about it except your conscience, I swear.'

'You swear?'

'Yes, I swear.'

This done, they took away the clothes they had given me and left me to put my own on again.

The dampness had affected me and I was in a critical state.

My body was covered with bruises and for several days I had only had a few drops of water and a little bread. I thought that would be the last persecution I would have to suffer. Thanks to the very short-lived effects of violent upheavals which prove how resilient nature is in the young, I recovered in no time, and when I reappeared it was to find the whole community convinced that I had been ill. I took up my domestic duties again and my place in church. I had not forgotten my document, nor the young sister to whom I had entrusted it, and I was sure that she had not misused what I had given her, but that she would not have kept it without misgivings. A few days after my release from prison, in choir at the very point in the service when I had given it to her – that is, when we kneel down and bow to those opposite, disappearing in our stalls – I felt my dress being gently pulled, held out my hand and she slipped me a note containing only these words: 'What a worry you have been to me! What am I to do with that dreadful paper?' After reading it I screwed the note up in my fingers and swallowed it. All this happened at the beginning of Lent and the time was approaching when interest in hearing the music draws to Longchamp the whole of Paris society, good and bad alike. I had a very good voice, and it had not deteriorated very much. In religious houses they pay attention to anything profitable, however small, so I was treated kindly in various ways, enjoyed a little more freedom, and the sisters I taught singing could risk contact with me. The sister to whom I had entrusted my document was one of these. During recreation time when we were in the garden I took her to one side, made her sing, and this is what I said while she was singing:

'You know lots of people and I know nobody. I should hate you to be compromised, and I would rather die here than expose you to the suspicion of having helped me. My dear friend, you would be ruined, I know, and it wouldn't save me; and even if your ruin could save me I wouldn't want to be saved at such a cost.'

'Never mind that,' she said. 'What can I do?'

'See that this draft reaches some skilful lawyer without his knowing which convent it comes from, and get an answer that you will give me in church or elsewhere.'

'By the way,' she said, 'what did you do with my note?'

'Don't worry, I swallowed it.'

'Don't you worry either. I will see what can be done for you.'

Note, Sir, that I sang while she was speaking and she sang while I answered her, so that our conversation was punctuated by bits of singing. This young person is still in the convent, Sir, her happiness is in your hands; if anyone should happen to find out what she did for me there is no describing the tortures she would be exposed to. I would not want to have opened the door of a prison cell for her, I would rather go back there myself. So burn these letters, Sir, for apart from the interest you are good enough to take in my fate they don't contain anything worth preserving.

That is what I told you then, but alas, she is no more, and I am left alone...

She quickly kept her word and informed me in our usual manner. Holy week came, and there was a huge crowd for Tenebrae. I sang well enough to provoke tumultuous bursts of that scandalous applause they give to actors in their theatres, and which should never be heard in the house of the Lord, above all during those solemn and mournful days when we honour the memory of His Son nailed to the Cross in atonement for the sins of all mankind. My young pupils had been well prepared, some had good voices and almost all some expressiveness and taste, and it seemed to me that the audience had heard them with pleasure and the community was satisfied with the success of my tuition.

You know, Sir, that on that Thursday the Blessed Sacrament is taken from its tabernacle to a special Easter sepulchre, where it remains until Friday morning. This interval is filled by perpetual adoration on the part of the nuns, who go to this sepulchre one by one or in pairs. A notice is put up indicating each one's hour of adoration, and how glad I was to read Sister Sainte-Suzanne and Sister Sainte-

Ursule from two in the morning until three. I went there at the stated time and my friend was there. We took up our positions side by side on the altar steps, we prostrated ourselves together and worshipped God for half an hour. At the end of that time my young friend took my hand and squeezed it, saying:

'We may never have a chance to talk as long and freely again. God knows the restrictions under which we live, and He will forgive us if we take up part of the time we should devote to Him alone. I have not read your memorandum, but it is not difficult to guess what is in it. I shall get an answer at any moment now. But if that reply authorizes you to proceed with the annulment of your vows, don't you see you will have to consult lawyers?'

'That is true.'

'For which you will need to be free?'

'True.'

'And that if you are wise you will take advantage of the present attitude towards you to get some freedom?'

'I had thought of that.'

'Will you?'

'I'll see.'

'And another thing: if your case is taken up you will be subjected to the full fury of the community here. Have you foreseen the persecutions in store?'

'They won't be any worse than those I have already been through.'

'I don't know about that.'

'Oh, but I do. First of all they won't dare to interfere with my liberty.'

'How do you know that?'

'Because by then I shall be under the protection of the law and I shall have to appear in person. I shall be, so to speak, between the world and the cloister, my mouth will be open and I shall be free to complain and call you all to witness. They won't dare put themselves in the wrong when I can complain about it, for they will take care that the case does not turn out badly for them. It would suit me very well if

they ill-treated me, but they won't – you can be sure that
they will adopt just the opposite line. They will plead with
me, pointing out the wrong I am about to do myself as
well as the convent, and you can be sure they won't resort to
threats until they have seen that sweetness and light are
useless, and forcible methods will not be allowed.'

'But it is incredible that you should have such distaste for
a way of life the duties of which you carry out so easily and
so scrupulously.'

'I recognize this distaste, which was born in me and will
never leave me. I should end by being a bad nun, and I
must forestall that.'

'But if you are unfortunate enough to lose?'

'If I lose I shall ask to be transferred, otherwise I shall die
in this convent.'

'People can suffer a long time before dying. Oh, my dear
friend, the step you are taking makes me shudder. I am
terrified that your vows will be annulled and also that they
will not. If they are, what will become of you? What will
you do in the world? You have good looks, intelligence and
talents, but it is said that these things lead nowhere if you
are virtuous, and I know that you will never be anything but
that.'

'You are doing justice to me, but not at all to virtue, and
it is on virtue that I rely. The rarer it is in mankind the
more highly it should be prized.'

'It is praised, but nothing is done for it.'

'It is virtue that is my help and encouragement in my
plans. Whatever exception is taken to me, my way of life
will be respected and at any rate it will not be alleged about
me, as it is about many others, that I am driven to abandon
my state by an uncontrollable passion. I see nobody and
know nobody. I am seeking to be free because the sacrifice
of my liberty was not freely made. Have you read my
memorandum?'

'No. I opened the package you gave me because it was not
addressed and I naturally thought it was for me, but the
first lines showed me I was wrong and I did not go on. How

well advised you were to give it to me! Another moment and it would have been found on you. But the end of our vigil is nearly here, and we must prostrate ourselves so that those who come to relieve us find us in our proper posture. Ask God to enlighten you and lead you. I will add my prayers and tears to yours.'

My soul was in some measure comforted. My companion prayed kneeling, but I bowed myself down, my forehead touching the bottom step of the altar and my arm stretching up the other steps. I don't think I have ever addressed God with more fervour and received more consolation; my heart palpitated violently and in a moment I lost all consciousness of anything round me. I don't know how long I stayed in that position or how long I might have stayed, but apparently I was a very touching sight to my companion and to the two nuns when they came. When I rose I thought I was alone, but I was mistaken, for the three of them were behind me and weeping; they had not dared to interrupt me, but had waited for me to emerge from the state of elation and ecstasy in which they saw me. When I turned back towards them the expression on my face must have been awe-inspiring to judge from the effect produced upon them at the time and from what they said later, namely that I looked like our former Superior when she used to console us and that my appearance had filled them with the same awe. If I had had any hypocritical or fanatical tendencies and had wanted to become a figure in the convent I am sure I should have been successful. My soul easily catches fire, becomes exalted and is deeply moved, and that saintly Mother Superior told me a hundred times that nobody would have loved God like me, for I had a heart of flesh and the others hearts of stone. It is true that I found it extremely easy to share her ecstasy, and when she prayed aloud I sometimes took up what she had said, went on with the thread of her thoughts and found as if by inspiration part of what she would have said herself. The others listened in silence or followed on what she had said, but I interrupted or even anticipated her or spoke with her. The impress I had taken from her remained stamped on me for a long time, and it seems that I must have given some of it back to her; for if it was clear in others that they had been conversing with her, it was also clear in her that she had been conversing with me. But what is the significance of all this if the vocation is not there? When our vigil was over we gave up our places to those who were to follow, and my young companion and I embraced very tenderly before separating.

This scene made a certain impression in the house, and to that you must add the success of Tenebrae on Good Friday, when I sang and played the organ and was applauded. Oh, the fickleness of nuns! I hardly needed to do anything in order to be welcomed back by the whole community – they met me more than half way, and the Superior was the first. Some people from the outside world wanted to make my acquaintance, and it all fitted in too well with my plans for me to refuse to meet them. I met the gentleman who was Presiding Magistrate, Madame de Soubise and many other worthy people, monks, priests, soldiers, magistrates, pious women and fashionable ones, and in addition those empty-headed fops called *red-heels*, whom I made short work of. I only encouraged those acquaintances nobody could object to, and handed the rest over to those nuns who were not so particular.

I forgot to mention that the first kind gesture to be made was my being allowed to return to my own cell. I made so bold as to ask to have back the miniature of our former Superior, and they had not the courage to refuse; it took its old place near my heart and there it will stay as long as I live. Every morning the first thing I do is lift up my heart to God, and the second is to kiss that picture. When I want to pray but my soul is cold, I take it from my neck and put it in front of me, look at it and it inspires me. It is a great pity that we never knew the saints whose images are placed for our veneration; they would make quite a different impression upon us and would not leave us so cold when we are at their feet or before them.

I had the answer to my memorandum; it came from a Monsieur Manouri, and it was neither favourable nor unfavourable. Before pronouncing on the matter he required a great deal of information which was difficult to give without a meeting, so I disclosed my name and invited him to come to Longchamp. These gentlemen are unwilling to travel about, but still he came. We had a long discussion and we agreed on a method of corresponding whereby he would be certain that his questions would reach me and I would send him my answers. All the time he was giving to my case I spent preparing people's minds, interesting them in my fate and getting introductions to influential people. I spread my name abroad, disclosed my behaviour in the first convent and what I had gone through in my parents' home, the trials I had had to undergo in the convent, my protest at Sainte-Marie and my stay at Longchamp, my taking the veil, my profession and the cruelty with which I had been treated since I had ratified my vows. I was pitied, I was offered help, and I held on to the goodwill shown towards me against the time when I might need it, but I did not go into any further explanation. Nothing transpired in the convent; I had obtained permission from Rome to appeal against my vows, the case was about to be heard at any moment, and still they were in blissful ignorance. So you can imagine the astonishment of my Superior when she was served with a notice of appeal against her vows in the name of Sister Marie-Suzanne Simonin, together with a request for permission to quit her religious habit, leave the convent and settle her own life as she might feel disposed.

Of course I had foreseen that I would encounter many kinds of opposition; from the law, from the religious house itself and from my brothers-in-law and sisters in their alarm. They had all the family money, and if I were free I should have a considerable claim to make on them. I wrote to my sisters and begged them not to oppose my leaving in any way, I appealed to their consciences about having had no freedom of choice over my vows, I offered to make a formal renunciation of any claims I had on my parents' estate, I spared no pains to persuade them that my action was not prompted by self-interest or passion. But I did not succeed in winning against their instincts: this legal act I was contemplating, being undertaken while I was still in religion, might become invalid, and it was too uncertain from their point of view that I would consider it binding when I was free; and besides, was it in their interests to agree to my proposals? Will they leave a sister with no home and no money? Will they enjoy her money? What will other people say? If she comes to us begging for bread, shall we refuse? If she takes it into her head to get married, who knows what kind of man she will have? And suppose she has children? No, we must thwart this dangerous plan with all our might and main ... That is what they said to themselves and what they acted on.

Scarcely had the Superior received the formal notice of my request than she rushed to my cell.

'What's this, Sister Sainte-Suzanne, do you want to leave us?'

'Yes, Reverend Mother.'

'And you are going to appeal against your vows?'

'Yes, Reverend Mother.'

'Did you not make them of your own free will?'

'No, Reverend Mother.'

'Then who forced you?'

'Everything.'

'Your father?'

'My father.'

'Your mother?'

'Yes, my mother herself.'

'Why did you not appeal at the altar?'

'I was so little in my right mind that I don't even remember having been there.'

'How can you say such things?'

'I am speaking the truth.'

'What? didn't you hear the priest ask you: Sister Sainte-Suzanne Simonin, do you promise to God obedience, chastity and poverty?'

'I have no recollection of it.'

'And do you imagine that people will believe what you say?'

'They can believe me or not, but the fact will be none the less true.'

'My dear child, if people listened to such tales think what abuses would follow! You have made a rash move, you have let yourself be carried away by a feeling of revenge, you are brooding over the punishment you forced me to inflict on you and which you think justified your breaking your vows. You are mistaken; that is not possible in the eyes of men nor of God. Reflect that perjury is the greatest of all crimes, and that you have already committed it in your heart and are on the point of doing so in fact.'

'I shall not be perjured, for I have sworn nothing.'

'If we are guilty of any wrongs against you, have they not been put right?'

'It is not any of these wrongs that have made me decide.'

'Then what is it?'

'Lack of vocation, no freedom of choice over my vows.'

'If you felt no vocation and if you were coerced, why didn't you say so at the proper time?'

'How would that have helped me?'

'Why didn't you show the same strength of purpose that you showed at Sainte-Marie?'

'Is strength of purpose in our control? I was strong the first time, but the second I was a fool.'

'Why didn't you consult a lawyer? Why not protest? You had the usual twenty-four hours in which to realize the mistake you had made.'

'Did I know anything about those formalities? Even if I had, was I in a fit state to have recourse to them? Supposing I had been in a fit state, could I have done so? Why, Madame, didn't you yourself notice the deranged state I was in? If I call you as witness will you swear that I was in my right mind?'

'Yes, I will!'

'Very well, Madame, then you will be the perjurer, not me.'

'My child, you are going to stir up a hornets' nest to no purpose. Take yourself in hand, I do beg of you, in your own interest and that of the convent; affairs like this never proceed without scandalous publicity.'

'That will not be my fault.'

'People out in the world are spiteful, and the most damaging conclusions will be drawn about your state of mind, your heart. They will believe...'

'Whatever they like.'

'But talk to me frankly, if you have some secret cause for dissatisfaction, whatever it may be, there is a way out.'

'I was, I am, and all my life I shall be dissatisfied with my lot.'

'Has the Evil One, who always prowls round us and seeks our perdition, been taking advantage of the excessive freedom you have been allowed recently in order to use his wiles to instil some wicked desire into your heart?'

'No, Reverend Mother, you know I never swear lightly, but I call God to witness that my heart is innocent and no shameful sentiment has ever dwelt there.'

'It is difficult to believe.'

'On the contrary, Madame, nothing is easier to believe. Each of us has a character, and I have mine. You love monastic life, and I hate it. God has given you the gifts of grace needed for your state, but I lack them all. You would have been lost in the world and here you are making sure of your own salvation, but I would be lost here and hope to save myself in the world. I am and always will be a bad nun.'

'But why? Nobody fulfils her duties better than you do.'

'But I do so with difficulty and against my inclinations.'

'You deserve greater things.'

'Nobody can know better than I do myself what I deserve, and I am forced to admit to myself that by being submissive I deserve nothing. I am tired of being a hypocrite, and by doing what saves others I hate and condemn myself. In a word, Madame, the only genuine nuns I know are those who are kept here by their taste for the retired life and who would stay even if they had no bars or walls to keep them in. I am far from being one of these; my body is here but my heart is not, it is out there, and if there had to be a choice between death and perpetual incarceration, I would not hesitate to die. Those are my sentiments.'

'What! would you abandon this veil and this habit which have set you apart for Jesus Christ, and have no remorse?'

'Yes, Madame, because I took them without proper thought and without freedom of . . .'

I answered her with a great deal of circumspection, for that was not at all what my heart wanted to say, which was: 'Oh for the days when I can tear them to pieces and fling them away!'

Nevertheless my answer appalled her; she went white, tried to say something else, but her lips were trembling and she had no idea what she wanted to say. I was striding up and down my cell, and she exclaimed:

'Oh Lord, what will our sisters say? Oh Jesus, turn a pitying eye upon her! Sister Sainte-Suzanne!'

'Yes, Madame?'

'So you have made up your mind? You mean to dishonour us, make us all the talk of the town, and bring about your own ruin!'

'I want to get out of here.'

'But if it is only the convent you don't like . . .'

'It is this convent, it is my condition, it is the religious life. I don't want to be shut up, either here or anywhere else.'

'My child, you are possessed of the devil. He it is who is making you act and speak, who is driving you mad. Nothing is more certain – look at the state you are in!'

I did look at myself, and indeed I saw that my dress was disordered, my wimple was turned round almost back to front and my veil had fallen down on to my shoulders. I was irritated by the words of this malicious Superior who for the purpose of speaking to me kept on using a honeyed and deceptive voice, and I said to her with some asperity:

'No, Madame, no, I don't want anything more to do with this habit, nothing more at all!'

And yet I was trying to readjust my veil, but my hands were shaking, and the more I tried to put it right the more I upset it, so that in exasperation I seized it roughly and tore it off and threw it on the ground. I stood there in front of my Superior with only a band round my forehead and my hair all over the place. All through this she was uncertain whether she should stay, and walked up and down saying:

'Oh Jesus, she is possessed! That is a certain fact, she is possessed!'

The hypocrite made the sign of the cross with her rosary.

I soon came to my senses, realizing the shocking state I was in and the imprudence of my words. I pulled myself together as best I could, picked up my veil and put it on again, then turned to her and said:

'Reverend Mother, I am neither mad nor possessed, but I am ashamed of my outburst and beg your forgiveness. You can, however, see from that how little the religious life suits me, and how right it is that I should seek to get out of it if I can.'

But she was not listening, merely going on repeating: 'What will people say? What will our sisters say?'

'Madame,' I said, 'if you want to avoid publicity there is one way. I am not trying to get my dowry back; all I ask is freedom. I don't suggest that you open the gates for me, but merely see to it that today, tomorrow or some time they are carelessly guarded, and don't notice my escape until as late as you can.'

'Wretched girl, what are you trying to suggest?'

'A piece of advice which a good and wise Superior should follow with all those for whom the convent is a prison, and for me it is an infinitely more horrible prison than those where criminals are kept, and I must get out of it or perish. Madame,' I went on in a solemn voice and looking her straight in the eye, 'listen. If the laws to which I have appealed prove to be unavailing, and if, in a fit of that despair I have already known all too often ... you have a well ... there are windows in this building ... there are walls facing one everywhere here ... one has a garment that can be torn into strips ... hands that can be used ...'

'Stop, you wretched girl! You make me shudder. What! Could you ...'

'Yes, I could, and if all the ways of making a quick end to the woes of life should fail, I could refuse food – we have the power to eat or drink or do neither ... If, after what I have just told you, it did happen that I had the courage – and you know I have no lack of it and that sometimes more courage is required to live than to die – transport yourself to the day of judgement and tell me which would appear the more guilty, the Superior or the nun? Madame, I am not asking for anything back from the convent, and I never shall; save me from a crime and yourself from lasting remorse ... let us work together ...'

'How can you think of such a thing, Sister Sainte-Suzanne? That I should fail in the first of my duties, be a party to crime and have a share in sacrilege!'

'The real sacrilege, Madame, is committed by me every day when, by my contempt, I profane the sacred habit I wear. Take it away from me, for I am unworthy of it, send for the rags of the poorest peasant woman in the village, and have the door left ajar.'

'And where will you go to be better off?'

'I don't know, but we are only badly off where God does not want us to be, and God does not want me to be here.'

'You have no money.'

'That is true, but poverty is not what I am most afraid of.'

'Beware of the excesses poverty drags you into.'

'The past guarantees the future, and if I had been inclined towards crime I should be free today. But if I decide that I must leave this establishment, it will be done either with your consent or by the authority of the law. You can choose ...'

This conversation had run on, and when I recalled it later I blushed at the unwise and silly things I had said and done, but it was too late. The Superior was still at the stage of exclaiming: 'What will people say? What will our sisters say!' when the bell for chapel sent us our various ways. As she left she said:

'Sister Sainte-Suzanne, you are going to the chapel; ask God to touch your heart and restore in you the spirit of your vocation. Consult your conscience and believe what it tells you; it is impossible for it not to reproach you. You are excused from singing.'

We went down almost together. The service came to an end, and when it was over and all the sisters were on the point of dispersing, she tapped on her breviary and stopped them.

'Sisters,' she said, 'I invite you to bow before the altar and implore God's mercy for a nun He has abandoned, who has lost her love of religion and its spirit, and is on the point of committing an act sacrilegious in the eyes of God and abhorrent to those of men.'

I cannot describe the general sensation; in an instant everyone, without herself moving, was searching the faces of her companions to try to identify the guilty one by her embarrassment. They all fell on their faces and prayed in silence. After a fairly long interval the Prioress softly intoned the *Veni Creator*, and all softly took it up. Then after another silence the Prioress tapped her desk and everybody went out.

I leave you to imagine the hubbub that arose in the community: 'Who is it? Who is it not? What has she done? What does she want to do? . . .' These suspicions did not last long. My request was beginning to be known in the outside world. I received endless visitors: some blamed me, others brought advice; I was approved of by some and censured by others. There was only one way I could justify myself in everybody's eyes and that was by informing them about my parents' behaviour, and you can see how careful I had to be on that subject. There were only a few persons, those who remained genuinely devoted to me, and Monsieur Manouri, who had taken on my case, in whom I could fully confide.

At times, when I was afraid of the comments I was threatened with, that dungeon into which I had been thrown once before rose in my imagination in its full horror. I knew what the malignity of nuns could be. I told Monsieur Manouri of my fears and he said: 'It is impossible to shield you from every kind of trouble; you will have troubles and you must expect them; you must arm yourself with patience and keep going on in the hope that they will come to an end. But as to that dungeon, I promise that you will never go back there again. I am seeing to that...' And indeed a few days later he served an order on the Superior that she had to produce me whenever she was requested to do so.

The following day after service I was again commended to the public prayers of the community. They prayed in silence and recited in a low voice the same hymn as the day before. The same on the third day, with this difference that I was ordered to stand in the middle of the choir and they recited the prayers for the dying, the litanies of the saints with the refrain *ora pro ea*. On the fourth day there was a pantomime typical of the weird mentality of the Superior. At the end of the service I was made to lie in a coffin in the centre of the choir, candles were placed on either side with a holy-water stoup, I was covered with a shroud and the prayers for the dead were recited, after which each nun, as she went out, sprinkled me with holy water and said *Requiescat in pace*. You have to be familiar with the language of convents in order to appreciate the particular threat implied in those last two words.* The nuns lifted the shroud, put out the candles and left me there, soaked to the skin with the water they had deliberately sprinkled over me. My clothes dried on me, for I had nothing to change into. This mortification was followed by another. A general assembly was held, I was treated as a delinquent, my action was designated as apostasy, and it was forbidden as an act of disobedience for any nun to speak to me, help me, come near me or even touch any object I had used. These orders

* See note on page 64. – *Trans.*

were strictly adhered to. Our corridors are narrow, and in some places it is difficult for two people to pass each other without turning sideways; if therefore I was going along and a nun came towards me, either she went back again or stood flat against the wall, clutching her veil and habit for fear of their touching mine. If anything had to be taken from me, I put it on the ground and they would pick it up with a cloth; if anything had to be given to me, they would throw it. If somebody had been unfortunate enough to touch me, she considered herself unclean and went to confess and obtain absolution from the Superior. Flattery has been called vile and mean; it is cruel and ingenious as well when it sets itself out to please somebody by inventing mortifications. How many times have I recalled the words of my saintly Mother de Moni: 'Among all these creatures you see round me, so docile, so innocent, so gentle, indeed, my child, there is scarcely one, yes, scarcely one, I could not turn into a wild beast, and the likelihood of this strange metamorphosis happening is the more marked the younger they go into a cell and the less they know of social life. This strikes you as a strange thing to say, and God save you from ever experiencing the truth of it. Sister Suzanne, the good nun is the one who brings with her into the cloister some grievous sin to expiate.'

I was deprived of all my functions. In church an empty stall was left on each side of mine. I sat alone at a table in the refectory, and nobody served me; I had to go and ask for my portion in the kitchen. The first time I went the cook shouted: 'Don't come in here, go farther away!'

I obeyed.

'What do you want?'

'Something to eat.'

'Something to eat! You aren't fit to live!'

Sometimes I came away and went all day without anything, but sometimes I insisted, and then they put down on the doorstep food one would have been ashamed to set before animals. I picked it up in tears and went away. If I happened to arrive last at the door of the choir I found it shut, and there I knelt down and waited for the end of the service, but if it was the door to the garden I went back to my cell. But my strength was being sapped by the lack of food and the poor quality of the food I had, and even more by the struggle I was having to bear so many repeated acts of inhumanity, and I felt that if I persisted in suffering without complaint I should never live to see the end of my lawsuit. So I made up my mind to speak to the Superior. I was half dead with panic, but I went and tapped softly on her door. She opened it and on seeing me stepped back several paces and cried:

'Apostate! keep away!'

I moved back.

'Farther.'

I moved farther away.

'What do you want?'

'Since neither God nor men have condemned me to death, I want you, Reverend Mother, to order that I be kept alive.'

'Alive!' she said, echoing the words of the cook, 'do you deserve it?'

'Only God knows that, but I am warning you that if I am refused food I shall be forced to make my complaint to those who have taken me under their protection. My stay here is only temporary until my fate and my standing have been decided.'

'Go away, and don't defile me by looking at me. I'll see to it.'

I went away and she slammed the door. Apparently she did give orders, but I was scarcely any better provided for. They made a point of disobeying her and threw me the most revolting food, and even then they spoilt it by mixing in ashes and all sorts of filth. That is the life I led while my case was going on. The parlour was not quite out of bounds because they could not take away my freedom to confer with my judges and lawyer, but even then the latter had to use threats more than once in order to see me. On these occasions I was accompanied by a nun, and she complained if I spoke too softly and grew impatient if I stayed too long; she interrupted, denied the truth of what I said, contradicted me, repeated what I had said to the Superior, changing and poisoning it and even inventing things I had not said at all, and so on. They did not stop at robbing me, stripping me, taking away my chairs, blankets and mattresses; I was given no more clean linen, my clothes were in rags and I was almost without shoes and stockings. I had trouble in getting water, and many times I had to go and find some myself at the well – that well I have told you about. They broke my utensils, and then I was reduced to drinking the water I had drawn up, having no means of taking any away. If I went past windows I had to quicken my steps or run the risk of receiving slops emptied from the cells. Some of the nuns spat in my face. I had become revoltingly dirty. As they were afraid I might complain to our spiritual directors I was forbidden to go to confession.

One Holy-day of Obligation, Ascension Day I think it was, my lock was put out of order and I could not go to Mass, and I should perhaps have missed other services had not Monsieur Manouri come to see me. At first he was told that they did not know what had become of me, nobody had seen me and I had given up all my Christian observances. But by dint of struggling I broke the lock and made for the door to the choir, which I found closed as was always the case if I was not one of the first to arrive. I lay sprawled on the ground with my head and back propped against one of the walls, my arms crossed over my breast and the rest of my body stretched across the passage and blocking it. When the service was over and the nuns appeared on their way out, the first one stopped dead, the others caught up with her and the Superior, guessing what it was, said:

'Walk over her, she's only a corpse now!'

Some of them obeyed and trampled on me, others were not so inhuman, but not one dared to give me a hand to help me up. During my absence they had taken away the prayer-stool from my cell, the portrait of our Founder and other religious pictures, with the crucifix; the only one I had left was the one on my rosary, and that was not to be with me for long. So I lived within four bare walls, in a room with neither door nor chair, either standing up or lying on a palliasse, without any of the most necessary vessels and forced to go out at night to satisfy the demands of nature, only to be accused in the morning of disturbing everybody's sleep, wandering about and going crazy. As my cell could not be shut now, they came crashing in during the night, shouting, jerking my bed, breaking my windows and doing all sorts of things to terrify me. The noise went up to the floor above and down to the one below, and those who were not in the conspiracy alleged that strange things were going on in my cell, that they had heard mournful voices, shoutings and the rattlings of chains, and that I held communion with ghosts and evil spirits, that I must have made a pact with the devil and that my corridor should be vacated at once.

There are weak heads in all enclosed communities, and they are even in the majority: those in our community believed what they were told, dared not pass my doorway; their troubled imaginations saw me with a hideous face, they crossed themselves when they passed me and fled shrieking: 'Satan, get thee hence! Lord, come to my aid!' One of the youngest was at the end of the corridor and I was going towards her, there was no way of avoiding me and she was seized with a terrible panic. First she turned her face to the wall and muttered in a shaky voice: 'My God, my God, Jesus, Mary!' But still I came on towards her, and when she felt me near she hid her face in her hands for fear of seeing me, leaped in my direction, hurtled right into my arms and yelled: 'Help! help! mercy! I am lost! Sister Sainte-Suzanne, have pity on me!' And with those words she fell back senseless on the floor.

Hearing her screams they rushed up and carried her away. I cannot tell how this incident was distorted, the most criminal-sounding story was made out of it, it was said that the demon of impurity had possessed me, and I was credited with intentions I dare not mention, and unnatural desires to which they attributed the obvious disarray of the young nun. Of course I am not a man, and I don't know what can be imagined about one woman and another, still less about one woman alone, but as my bed had no curtains and people came in and out of my room at all hours, what can I say, Sir? For all their circumspect behaviour, their modest eyes and the chastity of their talk, these women must be very corrupt at heart – anyway they know that you can commit indecent acts alone, which I don't know, and so I have never quite understood what they accused me of, and they expressed themselves in such veiled terms that I never knew how to answer them.

If I insisted on going into all the details about my persecutions I should never end. Oh Sir, if you have any children let my fate be a warning of the sort of fate you prepare for them if you let them go into the religious life without showing the strongest and most unmistakable signs of a vocation. What injustice there is in a world which allows a child to dispose of his own liberty at an age when he is not allowed to touch a penny. Kill your own daughter rather than imprison her in a cloister against her will – yes, kill her! How often have I wished that my mother had strangled me at birth! It would have been less cruel of her. Would you believe that they took away my breviary and forbade me to pray to God? I did not obey, as you can well imagine. Alas, it was my sole consolation; I lifted my arms to heaven and cried aloud, daring to hope that my cries were heard by the only Being who saw all my distress. They listened outside my door, and one day when I was calling upon Him out of the depth of my woe and imploring His help they said:

'You are calling upon God in vain; there is no God for you any more. Die in despair and be damned!'

Others added: 'Amen to that, apostate! Amen to that!'

But here is something that will appear stranger to you than anything else. I don't know whether it was an effect of spitefulness or illusion, but although nothing I did sug-

gested a deranged mind, and even less a spirit possessed of
the devil, yet they deliberated among themselves whether I
should be exorcized, and it was concluded by a majority
that I had renounced my baptism and anointing, that the
demon was dwelling in me and keeping me away from
divine service. One of them added that at certain prayers I
gnashed my teeth, that I had shuddering fits in chapel and,
furthermore, that at the elevation of the Blessed Sacrament
I wrung my hands. Another that I trampled the crucifix
underfoot and no longer wore my rosary (as a matter of fact
it had been stolen), that I uttered blasphemies I dare not
repeat to you. All agreed that something unnatural was
going on inside me, and that the Vicar-General should be
advised. This was done.

The Vicar-General was a Monsieur Hébert, a man of
some age and experience, sharp of tongue but just and
wise. He was told all about the unrest in the convent, which
was certainly considerable, but it is also certain that if I was
the cause I was an innocent one. You will of course suspect
that they did not omit from the memorandum they sent
him my nocturnal wanderings, my absences from choir, the
hubbub in my room, what one had seen and another heard,
my revolt against holy things, my blasphemies, the obscene
acts imputed to me, and as for the adventure of the young
nun, they made everything they wanted out of that. The
accusations were so serious and so numerous that, level-
headed though he was, Monsieur Hébert could not help
being to some extent taken in and thinking there must be a
good deal of truth in them. The affair struck him as important enough for him to investigate for himself; he noti-
fied the convent of his visit and did in fact come, with two
young priests who had been assigned to him and helped
him in his arduous functions.

A few days before this I heard someone coming quietly
into my room in the middle of the night. I said nothing,
but waited to be spoken to, and a soft and tremulous voice
called me:

'Sister Sainte-Suzanne, are you asleep?'

'No I am not. Who is it?'

'Me.'

'Who?'

'Your friend. I am frightened to death and risking disaster to give you some advice which may be useless. Listen, there is to be a visitation by the Vicar-General tomorrow or later. You will be accused, so think out your defence. Goodbye, courage, and the Lord be with you.'

Having said that she slipped away as noiselessly as a shadow.

You see, everywhere, even in religious houses, there are a few compassionate souls whom nothing can harden.

Meanwhile my case was causing considerable excitement, a crowd of people of all walks of life, both sexes and all callings, and quite unknown to me, took an interest in my fate and intervened on my behalf. You were among them, and perhaps the story of my case is better known to you than to me, because towards the end I could no longer confer with Monsieur Manouri. He was told that I was ill, he suspected he was being deceived and he was afraid I had been thrown into that dungeon again. He went to the Archbishop's palace where they did not deign to listen to him, for they had been warned that I was mad and probably something worse. He went back to the judges and insisted upon the carrying out of the order given to the Superior to produce me alive or dead whenever she was required to do so. The civil judges broached the matter with the ecclesiastical judges, who realized the consequences non-compliance with this order might have, and apparently it was this that hastened the visitation by the Vicar-General, for these personages, sick and tired of the endless squabbles in convents, are not usually in a great hurry to get involved in them. They know from experience that their authority is always evaded or whittled down.

I took advantage of my friend's warning and asked for God's help, composed myself and prepared my defence. All I prayed for was the boon of being interrogated and heard impartially, and it was granted, but you will hear at what a price. If it was to my interest to appear innocent and good before my judge, it was no less important for my Superior that I should seem to be wicked, possessed of the devil, guilty and insane. So while I was redoubling my fervour and prayers, they multiplied their spiteful tricks: I was given just enough food to prevent my dying of starvation, I was overwhelmed with mortifications and surrounded with more and more terrors, I was prevented from sleeping all night long, and everything that can ruin health and unhinge the mind was called into play with a refinement of cruelty you cannot imagine. You can get an idea from one example.

One day as I was leaving my cell for chapel or elsewhere I saw some tongs on the floor, lying across the passage. I bent down to pick them up and put them where they could easily be found by whoever had mislaid them. The light prevented my seeing that they were almost red-hot. I seized them, but when I dropped them again they tore all the skin off the palm of my hand. At night, in places where I had to walk, they left obstacles either in the way of my feet or at head-height, and I was hurt time after time; I wonder I was not killed. I had no light and had to move along cautiously with my hands held out in front of me. Broken glass was strewn for me to walk on. I was determined to report all this, and I kept more or less to my resolve. I found the door to the convenience locked and had to go down several floors and out to the end of the garden when the garden door was open, and when it was not ... Oh Sir, what evil creatures segregated women are; they are sure to give support to the hatred of their Superior and believe they are serving God by driving you to desperation! It was high time for the Archdeacon to arrive, and it was time for my case to be decided.

This was the most terrible moment of my life. For bear in mind, Sir, that I had no idea in what colours I had been painted in the eyes of this priest, and that he had come out of curiosity to see a girl possessed, or who was pretending to be so. The nuns thought that only an overwhelming terror could give rise to such a state in me, and this is how they set about producing it.

Early in the morning on the day of his visit the Superior came into my room, accompanied by three nuns, one carrying a holy water stoup, another a crucifix and the third some rope. The Superior said in a loud and fierce voice:

'Get up. Kneel down and commend your soul to God.'

'Reverend Mother,' I said, 'before obeying you, could I ask you what is to become of me, what you have decided for me and what I am to ask God for?'

My whole body broke into a cold sweat, I was shaking and felt my knees giving way. I stared in horror at her three dread companions, who were standing in line with stern faces, tight lips and eyes closed. Fear had separated each word of the question I had asked. Thinking from the continued silence that I had not been heard, I began once again the last words of the question, for I had not the strength to repeat it all, so said in a low and faint voice:

'What favour am I to ask God for?'

The answer was:

'Ask forgiveness for the sins of your whole life; speak as though you were at the moment of appearing before Him.'

These words led me to believe that they had taken counsel together and resolved to get rid of me. I had heard that that did sometimes occur in certain religious establishments – they judged, condemned and executed. I did not think that this inhuman method of trial had ever been used in a women's convent, but there were so many things I had never guessed and which did happen! This thought of imminent death made me want to cry out, but though my mouth was open no sound came. I moved towards the Superior with my arms held out in supplication and my body leaning backwards, swooning. I fell, but it was not a heavy fall. In such fainting fits when one's strength abandons one, the limbs seem to give way and as it were fold up unawares; nature, unable to hold up, seems to try to collapse gently. I lost consciousness and the sense of feeling, and merely heard confused and distant voices buzzing round me; whether it was real speech or a singing in my ears, I could make out nothing but this continual buzzing. I don't know how long I stayed in this condition, but I was dragged out of it by a sudden coldness which made my body jerk slightly and drew from me a deep sigh. I was soaked with water which had been poured over my body from a big holy water stoup. I was lying on my side in this puddle of water, with my head against the wall, mouth half-open and eyes glazed and half closed. I tried to open them and look about me, but it seemed as though I was surrounded by a thick haze through which I could only glimpse moving bits of garments, which I tried in vain to look at properly. I made an effort with the arm which was not supporting me, wanted to raise it, but it was too heavy. Yet my extreme weakness did gradually diminish, and I raised myself, supported my back against the wall with my two hands in the water and my head drooping on my chest, uttering occasional inarticulate and painful moans. These women stared at me with an expression suggesting that they were under compulsion, hence immovable, which deprived me of the courage to try to soften them. The Superior said:

'Stand her up.'

They seized me under the arms and lifted me up. She went on:

'Since she refuses to commend herself to God, so much the worse for her. You know what you have to do; do it.'

I had thought that the ropes they had brought were to strangle me with, and as I looked at them my eyes filled with tears. I asked for the crucifix to kiss and they refused to give it to me. I asked for the ropes to kiss, and they were held out to me. I stooped and took the Superior's scapulary, kissed it and said:

'My God, have mercy on me! My God, have mercy on me! Dear sisters, try not to hurt me too much.'

And I offered my neck.

I couldn't describe what happened to me or what they did

to me. It is known that people being led to execution – and I believed that was happening to me – are virtually dead before being executed. I found myself on the matting that served as a bed, with my arms tied behind my back, sitting up, with a big iron crucifix on my lap...

... Sir, I do realize all the trouble I am causing you, but you did want to know whether I was in any way deserving of the compassion I am expecting from you...

It was then that I felt the superiority of the Christian faith over all the other religions of the world; what profound wisdom there was in what blind philosophy calls the folly of the cross. In the state I was in what would have been the use to me of the vision of a successful legislator crowned with glory? I saw that innocent man, his side pierced, his brow crowned with thorns, his hands and feet pierced with nails and expiring in agony, and I said to myself: 'That is my God, and yet I dare to complain!' I clung to this idea and felt consolation revive in my heart. I saw the pointlessness of life and was only too happy to lose it before I had time to add to my sins. Yet I counted my years, realized I was barely twenty, and sighed. I was too weak, too cast down for my mind to rise above the terror of death; in full health I think I would have found more courage to be firm.

By now the Superior and her myrmidons had returned, and they found I had more command of myself than they expected or would have liked. They stood me up, put my veil down over my face, two seized me under the arms, the third pushed me from behind and the Superior gave me marching orders. I moved without knowing where I was going, but thinking it was to execution, I said. 'Oh God, have pity on me! Oh God, give me strength! My God, do not abandon me! Forgive me if I have given offence!'

I reached the chapel. The Vicar-General had celebrated Mass. The whole community was assembled. I was almost forgetting to tell you that, when I was in the doorway, these three nuns who were escorting me jostled and pushed me about violently, and appeared to be struggling with me, some dragging me by the arms while others were pulling me back from behind, as though I were resisting or reluctant to enter the chapel, which was not the case at all. I was led towards the altar steps: I could hardly hold myself up but was dragged on my knees as though I had refused to take up that position, and they held on to me as though I was intending to run away. The *Veni Creator* was sung, the Blessed Sacrament was exposed and benediction given. At the moment in benediction when all bow in veneration, those who had seized me by the arms bent me down as though by force, while others pressed their hands down on my shoulders. I felt these different movements, but it was impossible for me to guess what their object was. Eventually all was made plain.

After benediction, the Vicar-General took off his chasuble and simply put on his alb and stole, then came forward to the altar steps where I was kneeling: he was flanked by the two priests, with his back to the altar on which the Blessed Sacrament was exposed, and facing me. He came to me and said:

'Sister Suzanne, stand up.'

The sisters holding me lifted me brutally, but others surrounded me and held me round the waist, as though afraid I would run away. He went on:

'Untie her.'

They did not obey, but pretended to be concerned with the awkwardness or even danger of letting me go. But I told you that this man was blunt, and he repeated in a loud, hard voice:

'Untie her.'

They obeyed.

My hands had scarcely been freed before I uttered a painful, sharp cry which made him turn pale, while the hypocritical nuns who were escorting me scattered as if in terror.

He recovered, the nuns came back as if in fear and trembling, but I stood still and he said:

'What is your trouble?'

My only answer was to show him both my arms; the rope with which they had bound them had almost eaten into the flesh, and they were purple with the blood which could not circulate and had become congested, and he concluded that my cry was caused by the sudden pain of the blood resuming its circulation. He said:

'Take off her veil.'

It had been sewn up in various places without my realizing it, and once again there was a great deal of fumbling and violence over something which only needed it because they had arranged it so. It was important that this priest should see me haunted, possessed or crazy. Anyhow, by dint of tugging they broke the thread in some places, the veil or my dress was torn in others, and I could be seen.

I have a striking face; my great suffering had changed it but taken nothing from its character. I have a voice which touches the heart and my expression bears the stamp of truthfulness. The combination of these qualities made a strong impression of pity on the two young acolytes, but the Archdeacon himself was a stranger to such sentiments; he was a just man but insensitive, one of those unfortunate enough to be born to practise virtue without knowing its charm; they do good, just as they reason, because they have an orderly mind. He took the end of his stole, placed it on my head and said:

'Sister Suzanne, do you believe in God the Father, Son and Holy Ghost?'

I answered:

'I do believe.'

'Do you renounce Satan and all his works?'

Instead of replying I suddenly leaped forward and uttered a loud scream, and the end of his stole came off my head. He was very upset, and his companions changed colour. Some of the nuns fled and the others, who were in their stalls, left them in an uproar. He made a sign for quiet, but he kept his eyes on me, expecting some extraordinary manifestation. I reassured him:

'Sir, it isn't anything; one of the nuns stuck something

sharp right into me,' and raising my arms to heaven I
added amid floods of tears:

'They hurt me just at the moment when you were asking
whether I renounced Satan and all his wiles, and I quite
understand why ...'

They all protested through the mouth of the Superior
that nobody had touched me.

The Archdeacon again placed the end of his stole on my
head and the nuns made as if to come near, but he signed
to them to keep away, and then once again asked me if I
renounced Satan and all his works, and I answered in a firm
voice:

'I renounce him, I renounce him ...'

He had a crucifix brought and presented it to me to kiss,
which I did on the feet, hands and the wound in the side of
the Christ.

He ordered me to worship it aloud. I placed it on the
ground and said on my knees:

'Oh God, my Saviour, You died on the cross for my
sins and for those of all mankind, I adore You. Grant me
the reward for the torments You suffered, drop on me one
drop of the blood You shed, that I may be purified. Forgive
me, oh Lord, as I forgive my enemies ...'

Then he said:

'Make an act of faith,' and I did so.

'Make an act of love,' and I did so.

'Make an act of hope,' and I did so.

'Make an act of charity,' and I did so.

I have no recollection of the terms in which they were
expressed, but I think they were obviously moving, for I
made several of the nuns sob and the two young priests
shed tears. The Archdeacon asked me in amazement where
I had found these prayers I had just recited.

I said:

'In the depths of my heart, for they are my thoughts and
feelings and I swear to God who hears us everywhere and
who is present on this altar, that I am a Christian and am
innocent. If I have committed offences, God alone knows

95

what they are and He alone has the right to call me to account and punish me...'

At these words he cast a terrible glance at the Superior.

The rest of that ceremony, during which the majesty of God had been insulted, the holiest things profaned and the minister of the Church mocked, came to an end and the nuns retired, all except the Superior, myself and the two young priests. The Archdeacon sat down, and taking out the memorandum against me that had been given him, he read it aloud and questioned me on the articles it contained:

'Why do you not go to confession?'

'Because I am prevented.'

'Why do you not approach the sacraments?'

'Because I am prevented.'

'Why do you not come either to Mass or the divine office?'

'Because I am prevented.'

The Superior tried to break in, but he said in his sharp tone:

'Be quiet, Madame... Why do you leave your cell at night?'

'Because I have been deprived of water, a water-jug and all the things necessary for the needs of nature.'

'Why is there noise in your dormitory and your cell?'

'Because they are busy preventing me from sleeping.'

The Superior tried to speak again, and for the second time he said:

'Madame, I have already asked you to keep quiet; you will answer when I question you ... What is this about a nun torn out of your hands and found lying on the floor of the corridor?'

'That was the result of the terror of me that had been instilled into her.'

'Is she a friend of yours?'

'No, Sir.'

'You have never been into her cell?'

'Never.'

'You have never done anything indecent to her or to any of the others?'

'Never.'

'Why have you been tied up?'

'I don't know.'

'Why can't your cell be shut?'

'Because I broke the lock.'

'Why did you do that?'

'So as to open the door and go to service on Ascension Day.'

'You showed yourself in chapel that day?'

'Yes, Sir.'

The Superior said:

'Sir, that is not true, the whole community –'

I broke in:

'– will assure you that the choir door was shut, that they found me lying in the doorway, that you ordered them to walk over me, which some of them did; but I forgive them, and you too, Madame, for having ordered it. I am not here to accuse anybody, but to defend myself.'

'Why have you no rosary or crucifix?'

'They have been taken away from me.'

'Where is your breviary?'

'It has been taken away.'

'Then how do you say your prayers?'

'I pray with my heart and soul, although I have been ordered not to pray.'

'Who gave you that order?'

'Madame...'

The Superior made as if to speak again.

'Madame,' he said, 'is it true or false that you ordered her not to pray? Say yes or no.'

'I believed, and I had every reason to believe...'

'That is not the point. Did you forbid her to pray, yes or no?'

'I forbade her, but...'

She was about to go on.

'But,' the Archdeacon broke in, 'but ... Sister Suzanne, why are you barefoot?'

'Because I have been given no shoes or stockings.'

'Why are your clothes in this worn and dirty state?'

'Because for over three months now I have been refused clean linen, and am forced to sleep with my clothes on.'

'But why sleep with your clothes on?'

'Because I have no curtains, mattresses, blankets, sheets or night-gowns.'

'Why not?'

'They have been taken away.'

'Are you properly fed?'

'I am asking to be.'

'So you are not?'

I said nothing, and he went on:

'It is incredible that you should have been so harshly treated without your having committed some offence to deserve it.'

'My offence is that I was not called to the religious life and that I am questioning vows I did not make of my own free will.'

'That is for the law to decide, and however it decides you must meanwhile fulfil the duties of the religious life.'

'Nobody, Sir, is more conscientious than I am.'

'You must share in the life of all your companions.'

'That is all I am asking for.'

'Have you no complaint against anybody?'

'No Sir. I have told you that I am not here to accuse, but to defend myself.'

'You may go now.'

'Where, Sir?'

'To your cell.'

I took a few steps, then turned back and threw myself at the feet of the Superior and the Archdeacon.

'Well,' he said, 'what is the matter?'

Displaying my head bruised in several places, my bleeding feet, my livid and fleshless arms, my dirty and torn clothes, I said:

'You can see!'

I can hear you. Sir, and most of those who read these memoirs, saying: 'So many horrors, so varied and so continuous! A series of such calculated atrocities in religious souls! It defies all probability.' I agree with you, but it is true, and I call on Heaven to judge me with all its severity and condemn me to eternal flames if I have allowed calumny to touch a single line of mine with its faintest shadow! Although I had prolonged experience of the extent to which a Superior's dislike can be a goad to natural perversity, especially when she could make a virtue out of it and congratulate herself and boast about her crimes, yet resentment will not prevent my being just. The more I reflect about it the more I am convinced that what was happening to me had never happened before and will perhaps never happen again. Once (and please God it was the first and last time) it pleased Providence, whose ways are baffling to us, to heap upon one unhappy creature the whole mass of cruelties previously shared, by its impenetrable decree, over the infinite multitude of poor wretches who had preceded her in a cloister or who were to succeed her. I have suffered, and suffered a great deal, but the fate of my persecutors seems to me, and has always seemed, more pitiable than mine. I would prefer to die, and would always have preferred it, than give up my role on condition that I play theirs. My troubles will come to an end, through your kindness I trust, but the shame and remorse of crime will stay with them to their last hour. They are already accusing themselves, you may rest assured; they will accuse themselves all through life, and terror will go down with them into the grave. Meanwhile, Monsieur le Marquis, my present situation is deplorable, life is a burden to me, I am a woman, and weak in spirit like others of my sex. God may abandon me, and I don't feel I have the strength or courage to bear much longer what I have borne. Sir, watch lest another fatal moment come, and should you wear out your eyes weeping over my doom, should you be torn asunder by remorse, it would not bring me back from the abyss into which I had fallen and which would close for ever over a lost soul.

•

'You may go now,' said the Archdeacon.

One of the priests gave me his hand to lift me up, and the Archdeacon added:

'I have questioned you and I am going to question your Superior, and I shall not leave this place until order has been restored.'

I went away. I found the rest of the convent in a commotion – all the nuns were at the doors of their cells and they were chattering from one side of the corridor to the other, but as soon as I appeared they retired, and there was a long drawn out noise of doors being slammed one after the other. I went back to my cell, knelt facing the wall and prayed God to have regard to the moderation with which I had spoken to the Archdeacon and make him see my innocence and the truth.

I was still praying when the Archdeacon, his two companions and the Superior appeared in my cell. I have told you that I had neither carpet nor chair, prayer-stool, curtains, mattress, blankets, sheets nor any utensils, nor a door that would shut and hardly a pane of glass intact in my windows. I rose to my feet, the Archdeacon stopped dead, and turning indignant eyes upon the Superior, said:

'Well, Madame?'

She answered:

'I didn't know.'

'You didn't know? You are lying! Have you ever let a single day pass without coming in here, and weren't you coming from here when you met me? Sister Suzanne, tell me, has not Reverend Mother been here today?'

I made no answer, and he did not insist, but the young priests dropped their arms and looked down as though their eyes were glued to the floor, which clearly revealed their embarrassment and surprise. They all left, and I heard the Archdeacon saying to the Superior in the corridor:

'You are unworthy of your functions, you deserve to be dismissed from your office. I shall lodge my complaint with the Bishop. All this disorder must be put right before I go.'

And while walking along he shook his head and said:

'It's horrible! Christians! Nuns! Human beings! Horrible!'

From that moment I heard no more, but I had linen again, fresh clothes, curtains, sheets, blankets, utensils, my breviary, my devotional books, rosary, crucifix and some new window-panes, in a word all the things which restored my normal position in the convent. Moreover I was given back the freedom of the parlour, but only for the discussion of my case.

This was not going well at all. Monsieur Manouri published a first memorandum which made little impression – there was too much intelligence and not enough pathos in it, and hardly any real arguments. But one cannot blame it altogether on this skilful advocate, for I absolutely refused to let him besmirch the good name of my parents, I wanted him to tone down his strictures on convent life, and especially on the house in which I was, and I did not want him to paint my brothers-in-law and sisters in too odious colours. All I had in my favour was that my first protestation, momentous it is true, had been made in a different convent and not been renewed since. When you set such narrow limits to your defence and have to deal with opponents who set none to their attack, who trample underfoot just and unjust alike, who make allegations or denials with the same aplomb and who blush neither at imputations, suspicions, gossip nor calumny, you can hardly expect to win, especially before courts in which habit and boredom hardly permit a properly scrupulous examination even of the most important cases, and in which cases of the nature of mine are always looked upon unfavourably by the politician who is afraid that, following the success of one nun appealing against her vows, a host of others will embark on the same project; for he feels in his heart of hearts that if the prison gates were once allowed to be thrown down in favour of one unhappy woman, the whole mob would hurl itself against them and try to force them. They try to discourage us and make us resigned to our fate through despair of ever changing it. Yet it seems to me that in a properly governed state it should be the opposite: difficult to enter into religion but easy to come out. And why not add this kind of case to so many others in which the slightest irregularity of form cancels the whole proceedings, however just they may otherwise be? Are convents so essential to the constitution of a state? Were monks and nuns instituted by Jesus Christ? Can the Church positively not do without them? What need has the Bridegroom of so many foolish virgins? And the human race of so many victims? Will they never realize the necessity for narrowing the entrance to these chasms into which future generations are going to plunge to their doom? Are all the routine prayers which are said there worth as much as the penny that charity gives to the poor? Does God, who made man sociable, approve of his hiding himself away? Can God, who made man so inconstant and frail, authorize such rash vows? Can these vows, which run counter to our natural inclinations, ever be properly observed except by a few abnormal creatures in whom the seeds of passion are dried up, and whom we should rightly classify as freaks of nature if the state of our knowledge allowed us to understand the internal structure of man as well as we understand his external appearance? Do all these lugubrious ceremonies played out at the taking of the habit or the profession, when a man or woman is set apart for the monastic life and for woe, suspend the animal functions? On the contrary, do not these instincts awaken in silence, constraint and idleness with a violence unknown to the people in the world who are busy with countless other things? Where do we see minds obsessed by impure visions which haunt them and drive them on? Where do we see that fathomless boredom, that pallor, that emaciation which are all symptoms of wasting and self-consuming nature? Where are nights troubled by groans and days bathed in tears shed for no reason and preceded by fits of melancholy for which no cause can be found? Where is it that nature, outraged at constraint for which she is not designed, breaks down the obstacles put in her way and in a frenzy of madness throws the working of our bodies into a disorganization beyond all curing? Where have irritation and temper destroyed all the social qualities? Where do neither father, brother, sister, relation nor friend exist? Where is it that man, considering himself as but a creature of a moment and gone tomorrow, treats the most affectionate relationships in this world as a traveller treats odd things he passes, with no attachment? Where is the dwelling-place of hatred, disgust and hysteria? Where is the place of servitude and despotism? Where are undying hatreds and passions nurtured in silence? Where is the home of cruelty and morbid curiosity? Nobody knows the story of these places, went on Monsieur Manouri in his argument, nobody knows. At another point he added: 'A vow of poverty means binding oneself on oath to be an idler and a thief, a vow of chastity means promising God continual breaking of the wisest and most important of His laws, a vow of obedience means giving up man's inalienable prerogative, freedom. If one observes these vows one is a criminal, if not one is a perjurer. The cloistered life is that of a fanatic or a hypocrite.'

A girl asked her parents' permission to enter our order. Her father said he consented, but gave her three years to think it over. This decree seemed hard to the girl, who was full of zeal, but she had to submit. However, her vocation having proved genuine, she came back to her father and said that the three years had gone by. 'That is very nice, my dear,' he answered, 'I granted you three years to test yourself, and now I hope you will be willing to grant me the same for making up my mind.' That seemed even harsher, and tears were shed, but the father was a determined man and he stuck to it. At the end of the six years she did come in and make her profession. She was a good nun, simple, pious and meticulous in all her duties. But what happened was that the confessors took advantage of her truthfulness in order to find out in the confessional what was going on in the convent. Our superiors guessed as much, so she was shut up, deprived of religious observances, and she went out of her mind, for how can a mind resist the persecutions of fifty people bent on tormenting it from morn till eve? Previously they had set a trap for her mother that well illustrates the greed of these establishments. They put into the head of this nun's mother the desire to come to the convent and visit her daughter in her cell. She applied to the Vicar-General, who granted the permission she sought. She arrived and hurried to her child's cell, but what was her amazement when she found nothing there but four bare walls! Everything had been taken away. It was calculated that this loving and impressionable mother would not leave her daughter in such conditions, and of course she refurnished the room, set her up again in clothes and linen, but protested to the nuns that her curiosity was too expensive for her to indulge in a second time, and that three or four such visits in a year would ruin the girl's brothers and sisters. This is the place where ambition and ostentation sacrifice one part of a family to secure a more comfortable life for the remainder, in fact the midden into which the refuse of society is thrown. How many mothers like mine expiate one secret crime with another!

Monsieur Manouri issued a second memorandum which had rather more effect. Great efforts were made, and once again I offered to cede to my sisters full and unquestioned possession of my parents' estate. There was one moment when my case took on a most favourable turn and I hoped for freedom, which made my disappointment all the more cruel, for my case was heard in court and lost. The whole community knew all about it but I was still in ignorance. There was much darting to and fro, hubbub, joy, little secret conclaves, comings and goings between the Superior's and each other's rooms. I was quite restless and unable to stay in my cell or go out, for there was not a single friend in whose arms I could seek comfort. What a dreadful morning that of the verdict of a big case is! I wanted to pray but could not, I fell to my knees and concentrated on a prayer, but soon my mind was wandering in spite of myself and I was in the midst of my judges; I could see them, hear the advocates, I spoke to them, interrupted my own counsel, finding my case badly argued. I did not know any of the magistrates, yet I visualized them in different ways, some favourable but some sinister and others nondescript. I was in an inconceivable mental ferment. The noise was followed by a complete silence, the nuns had stopped talking to each other. It seemed that their voices in the choir were more brilliant than usual – that is those who sang, for others did not sing and slipped away in silence when the service was over. I persuaded myself that the suspense was worrying them as much as me, but in the afternoon the noise and movement suddenly started again everywhere; I heard doors opening and shutting, nuns coming and going, the murmur of people talking softly. I kept my ear to the keyhole, but people seemed to stop talking as they went past and walked on tiptoe. I had a premonition that I had lost my case, indeed I did not doubt it for a moment. I began silently pacing round and round my cell, I felt stifled, I could not cry, but crossed my arms above my head and supported my head against one wall or the other. I wanted to rest on my bed, but could not for the beating of my heart – it is certain that I could even hear my heart beating, and see it making my dress palpitate too. I was in that condition when I was told that I was wanted. I went down, hardly daring to breathe! The nun who had fetched me was so gay that I thought the news brought for me could only be depressing, but still I went. When I reached the parlour door I stopped dead and shrank into the corner between the two walls, I could hardly stand up, yet I went in. There was nobody there; I waited but they had prevented the man who had asked for me from getting there first, for they felt sure he would be a messenger from my advocate and, wanting to know what passed between us, they had gathered together to listen. When he appeared, I was seated with my head resting on my arm and supported against the bars of the grille.

'This is from Monsieur Manouri,' he said.

'It will be to inform me that I have lost my case.'

'Madame, I know nothing about that, but he gave me this letter. He looked very upset when he gave it to me, and I have come post haste as he asked me to do.'

'Give it to me.'

He held out the letter, which I took without moving and without looking at it. I put it down on my lap and stayed like that. But he asked me: 'Is there no answer?'

'No,' I said, 'you can go.'

He went away and I stayed there, unable to move or make up my mind to leave.

We are not allowed to write or receive letters in a convent without the Superior's permission, and both letters received and written are submitted to her, so I had to take mine. I set out to do so, but I thought I should never get there; a condemned man leaving his dungeon to hear his sentence could not be slower or more cast down. However, I reached her door. The nuns looked on from a distance, anxious not to miss any of the spectacle of my grief and humiliation. I knocked, the door opened. The Superior was there with some of the nuns, as I knew from seeing the bottom of their garments, for I dared not raise my eyes. I presented my letter with a trembling hand; she took it, read it and handed it back to me. I returned to my cell and threw myself on the bed. The letter was beside me, but I stayed there without reading it, without getting up for dinner, without making a single movement until the afternoon service. At half past three the bell summoned me to go down. A few nuns were already there, the Superior was at the entrance to the choir, she stopped me and ordered me to stay outside on my knees; the rest of the community went in and the door was shut. After the service they all came out; I let them pass and rose to follow at the end. From that time I began to submit to anything they wanted – they had cut me off from church, so I cut myself off from refectory and recreation. I looked at my situation from all angles, and I could see no sort of alleviation except through their need of my talents and in my submission. I would have been content with the sort of oblivion I was left in for several days. A few visitors called, but Monsieur Manouri was the only one I was allowed to see. When I went into the parlour I found him in exactly the same posture as I had been when I received his emissary: head resting on arms and arms supported against the grille. I saw him but said nothing. He dared not look at me nor speak to me directly.

'Madame,' he said, without changing his position. 'I wrote to you; have you read my letter?'

'I received it, but I haven't read it.'

'So you don't know ...'

'Yes, Sir, I know everything. I have guessed what my fate is, and I am resigned.'

'How are they treating you?'

'So far they haven't thought of me at all, but the past tells me what the future has in store. I have but one consolation, which is that without the hope that has kept me going I cannot possibly suffer as much as I have suffered already, for I shall die. The offence I have committed is not one of those they overlook in the religious life. I am not asking God to soften the hearts of those to whose discretion it pleases Him to abandon me, but to grant me strength to suffer, save me from despair and call me quickly to Himself.'

'Madame,' he said, and he was weeping, 'even if you had been my own sister I couldn't have done more.'

This man has a kind heart.

'Madame,' he went on, 'if I can be of any help to you do please make use of me. I will see the First President, who thinks well of me, I will see the Vicars-General and the Archbishop.'

'Sir, see nobody, it is all over.'

'But if we could arrange for you to change convents?'

'There are too many obstacles in the way.'

'But what sort of obstacles?'

'Permission is very difficult to obtain, there would be a new dowry to be found, or the old one to be recovered from this place, and besides, what shall I find in a new convent? My own inflexible heart, pitiless Superiors, nuns no better

than those here, the same duties, the same troubles. Better
that I should end my days here; they will be shorter.'

'But, Madame, you have interested many worthy people,
and most of them are wealthy; they won't hold you here if
you leave without taking anything away with you.'

'So I believe.'

'A nun who leaves or dies adds to the comfort of the
remainder.'

'But these worthy and rich people have already forgotten
all about me, and you will find them very lukewarm when it
is a matter of endowing me at their own expense. Why do
you suppose it would be easier for people outside to help a
nun with no vocation to leave the cloister than for pious
souls to help one with a genuine vocation to go in? Is it so
easy to find dowries for the latter? No, Sir, since I lost my
case everybody has melted away, and I can't see anybody
left.'

'Madame, just leave this business to me, and I shall be far
happier.'

'I ask for nothing, hope for nothing, object to nothing,
my only incentive to live is gone. If only I could be sure
that God would change me, and that the qualities necessary
for the religious life would replace the hope of leaving it
which I have now lost! But it cannot be, and this nun's
habit has attached itself to my skin and bones, and irks me
all the more. Oh, what a fate! To be a nun for ever and feel
that one can never be anything but a bad one! To spend
one's whole life battering one's head against prison bars!'

At this point I began screaming. I tried to stifle it, but in
vain. Monsieur Manouri was amazed at this outburst, and
said:

'Madame, dare I ask you a question?'

'Do, Sir.'

'Could there be some secret reason for such overwhelming grief?'

'No, Sir. I loathe the solitary life, I feel here in my heart
that I loathe it, that I always shall. I can never submit to all
these trivial occupations that fill the day of a recluse, it is a

tissue of puerilities that I despise. I would have got used to it by now if I had been capable of doing so – I have tried a hundred times to deceive myself and break my own resistance, but I cannot. I have envied the blissful vacuity of mind of my companions, and implored God for it, but it has not been vouchsafed and He will not give it. I do everything badly and say everything wrong, lack of vocation shows through everything I do and is clearly visible. At every turn I am an insult to the monastic life, my inability to do things is labelled pride and they are bent on humiliating me: offences and punishments are multiplied for ever, and my days are spent measuring the height of walls with my eyes.'

'Madame, I can't knock them down for you, but I can do something else.'

'Sir, don't try anything.'

'You must change convents, and I will see to it. I shall come and see you again, and I hope they won't keep you concealed. You will hear from me very soon. Rest assured that if you are willing, I shall succeed in getting you out of here. If they treat you too harshly don't leave me in ignorance about it.'

It was late when Monsieur Manouri left. I returned to my cell. The bell soon rang for evening service. I was one of the first to arrive, and I let the nuns go in, taking it as settled that I should have to stay at the door, and in effect the Superior shut me out. That evening at supper she signalled to me to sit on the floor in the middle of the refectory, which I did, and was given nothing but bread and water. I ate a little and wept. The next day they held a conclave, and the whole community was called on to judge me. I was condemned to go without recreation, to hear the service from the choir door for a month, to eat on the floor in the middle of the refectory, to make a public confession of guilt for three days running, and to enact over again my taking the habit and my vows, wear the hair-shirt, fast every other day and scourge myself after evening service every Friday. While this sentence was being pronounced I was kneeling, with my veil lowered.

Next day the Superior came to my cell accompanied by a nun carrying over her arm a hair-shirt and the coarse garment I had been dressed in when I was put into the dungeon. I understood what this meant, so I undressed, or rather my veil and clothes were torn off me, and I put on this garment. My head was uncovered and I was barefoot, my long hair fell over my shoulders, and my whole clothing consisted only of this hair-shirt I had been given, a very coarse chemise and the long garment which came up to my neck and reached down to my feet. That was how I was dressed all day and how I appeared at all religious exercises.

That evening, after I had retired to my cell, I heard a procession approaching, singing litanies – it was the whole convent in double file. Some of them came in, I stood ready, a rope was put round my neck, a lighted torch in one hand and a scourge in the other. One nun took the end of the rope and I was led between the two rows and the procession set off for a little inner oratory dedicated to St Mary. They had come singing softly, but returned in silence. When I had reached this little oratory, which was lit by two lamps, I was ordered to beg the forgiveness of God and the community for the scandal I had caused; the nun who was leading me told me in a whisper what I had to repeat, and I did so word for word. After that the rope was taken off and I was undressed down to the waist, my hair, which had been over my shoulders, was pulled to one side of my neck, the scourge I had been carrying in my left hand was put into my right, and they began the *Miserere*. I realized what was expected of me and I did it. When the *Miserere* was over the Superior gave me a short exhortation, the lamps were put out, the nuns retired and I put my clothes on again.

When I got back to my cell I felt terrible pains in my feet, I looked down and saw that they were covered in blood from cuts made by bits of glass they had spitefully thrown in my path.

I made my public confession of guilt in the same way on both the following days, only on the last day they added a Psalm to the *Miserere*.

The Nun

On the fourth day my nun's habit was returned to me with approximately the same ceremonial as is devoted to this solemnity when it is done in public.

On the fifth I renewed my vows. For a month I fulfilled the rest of the penance imposed on me, and thereafter I more or less returned to my place in the normal routine of the establishment. I went back to my old position in the choir and refectory and took my turn in the various functions of the house. But what was my surprise when I looked at that young friend who had been so interested in my fate! She seemed almost as changed as I was, she was terrifyingly thin and her face bore the pallor of death, her lips were bloodless and her eyes almost unseeing.

'Sister Ursule,' I whispered, 'what is wrong with you?' 'Wrong with me?' she answered, 'I love you, and you ask me that! It was high time your ordeal ended, for it would have killed me.'

The reason why my feet had not been cut on the last two days of my public confession was that she had been careful to sweep the corridor stealthily and so move the bits of glass to either side. On the days when I was condemned to fast on bread and water she went without part of her portion, which she wrapped in a clean white cloth and threw into my cell. They had chosen by ballot which nun should lead me by the rope, and it had fallen to her, but she had the strength of character to go to the Superior and protest that she would rather face death than perform this unspeakable and cruel function. Fortunately she came from a distinguished family and enjoyed a handsome allowance which she used in accordance with the Superior's wishes, and so, at the cost of a few pounds of sugar and coffee, she found a nun to take her place. I would not presume to think that that unworthy woman had been struck by the hand of God, but she went out of her mind and is now shut up; the Superior is alive, governs, tortures and is in excellent health.

My health could not hold out against such prolonged and harsh ordeals, and I fell ill. It was at this juncture that Sister Ursule showed the full extent of her friendship for me. I owe her my life. Not that that was a good thing to preserve for me, as she sometimes told me herself; nevertheless there were no kinds of services she did not render on the days when she was on nursing duty, and even on the other days I was not neglected, thanks to the interest she took in me and the little rewards she handed out to those looking after me, according to how pleased I was with them. She had asked permission to nurse me at night, but the Superior had refused, alleging that she was too delicate to stand up to the fatigue, and it was a real sorrow to her. But all her devotion failed to halt the progress of the illness, and I was soon at death's door and received the last sacraments.

A few minutes earlier I had asked to see the whole assembled community, and this was granted. The nuns stood round my bed, the Superior among them. My young friend was at my bedside holding one of my hands which she moistened with her tears. They presumed I had something to say, so I was raised into a sitting posture, with two pillows supporting me. Then I addressed the Superior and begged her to give me her blessing and forget any offence I had given. I asked forgiveness from all my companions for the scandal I had brought upon them. I had had placed beside me a number of little treasures – things which adorned my cell or were for my personal use – and I asked the Superior's permission to give these away, which she granted, and I gave them to the nuns who had acted as assistants when I was thrown into the dungeon. I asked the one who had dragged me by the rope on the day of my public confession to come to me, and I embraced her and gave her my rosary and crucifix, and said: 'Beloved sister, remember me in your prayers and be assured that I shall not forget you before God.' Why did God not take me at that moment? I was going to Him without fear. That is such a great boon, and who can expect it twice? Who knows what I shall be like at my last moment? For I shall have to come to it. May God renew my troubles and give me that moment as tranquil as it was then! I saw the heavens opening out before me, and they assuredly were, for conscience does not deceive us at such a time, and conscience promised me eternal bliss.

After receiving the last rites I fell into a kind of lethargy, and they despaired of my life all that night. Now and again somebody came and felt my pulse; I was conscious of hands exploring my face and heard different voices saying afar off: 'It's going up again ... Her nose is cold ... She won't last until tomorrow ... The rosary and crucifix will be yours...' And another voice saying angrily: 'Go away, go away and let her die in peace, haven't you tortured her enough?' It was a very sweet moment for me, when I emerged from this crisis, opened my eyes and found myself in my friend's arms. She had never left me and had spent the whole night assisting me, repeating the prayers for the dying, making me kiss the crucifix and putting it to her own lips when she had taken it from mine. When she saw me open my eyes wide and heave a deep sigh she thought it was the end, and began to cry aloud, calling me her friend. She said: 'My God, have pity on her and me! My God, receive her soul! Dearest friend, when you are before God, remember Sister Ursule...' I looked at her with a sad smile, wept and squeezed her hand.

At that moment Monsieur Bouvard, the convent doctor, arrived. This man is skilful, so they say, but autocratic, arrogant and hard. He roughly pushed my friend away, felt my pulse and skin. He was accompanied by the Superior and her favourites. He asked a few monosyllabic questions about what had happened, and concluded: 'She'll get over it.' Then looking at the Superior, whom this verdict did not please, he went on: 'Yes, Madame, she'll get over it; the skin is healthy, the temperature has come down and some life is coming back into her eyes.'

With each of these remarks joy spread on the face of my friend, and on that of the Superior and her companions a sort of annoyance ill disguised by decorum.

'Sir,' I said, 'I don't want to live.'

'I can't help that!' he said, and then prescribed something and went off. It is said that while I was comatose I had said several times: 'Dear Mother, so I am going to join you! I will tell you everything.' Apparently I was addressing my former Superior; I am sure I was. I did not give her miniature to anybody, meaning to take it with me into the grave.

Monsieur Bouvard's forecast proved true; the temperature went down thanks to abundant sweating, and my recovery was now certain, and in effect I did recover, but had a very long convalescence. It was ordained that in that establishment I should suffer all the ills it is possible to go through. My illness was infectious, and Sister Ursule had scarcely ever left my side. When I was beginning to recover my strength hers was declining, her digestion was upset, and in the afternoon she was taken with fainting fits lasting sometimes up to a quarter of an hour: when she was in that condition she seemed dead, her sight grew dim, her brow was covered with a cold sweat which accumulated and ran in drops down her cheeks, her arms hung loose at her sides. The only way she could be given some slight relief was by unlacing her and loosening her clothing. When she came out of one of these faints her first thought was to look for me at her side, where she always found me, and sometimes even, when she still had a little feeling and consciousness left, she would feel round with her hand without opening her eyes. This gesture was so clear in its meaning that when various nuns had offered themselves to this groping hand and not been recognized, because she had then gone inert, they said to me: 'Sister Suzanne, it's you she wants, come nearer ...' I threw myself down by her and moved her hand to my forehead, where it stayed until she came out of her faint, and when it was over she said: 'Well, Sister Suzanne, I am the one who is going away and you will stay. I shall be the first to see her, I shall tell her about you and she will not hear me without weeping. There may be bitter tears, but there are also sweet ones, and if there is love in Heaven why not tears?' She put her head on my shoulder, wept copiously and then went on: 'Good-bye, Sister Suzanne, good-bye my dear friend. Who will share your troubles when I am no longer there to do so? Who will...? Oh, my dear, I pity you! I am going, I can feel I am, I am going. If you were happy what regrets I should have at dying!'

Her condition appalled me. I spoke to the Superior about it, for I wanted her to be moved into the infirmary and to be excused from chapel and the other irksome domestic duties. Also I wanted a doctor to be sent for, but the reply always was that it was nothing, that these attacks would pass off of their own accord, and that dear Sister Ursule was only too anxious to fulfil her obligations and follow the normal routine. One day, after Matins, which she had attended, she failed to reappear. I thought she must be very ill, and as soon as the morning services were over I rushed to her room and found her lying on her bed fully dressed. She said: 'Oh, there you are, dear friend, I felt sure you would not be long and I was expecting you. Listen. How impatient I was for you to come! My attack was so bad and lasted so long that I thought I should never recover and should never see you again. Look, here is the key of my oratory; open the cupboard and remove a little partition which divides the lower drawer into two. Behind this partition you will find a bundle of papers that I have never been able to make up my mind to part with, though it was dangerous to keep them and upsetting to read them. Alas, they are almost blotted out by my tears. When I am no more you must burn them.'

She was so weak and so exhausted that she could not pronounce two words of this speech consecutively, but stopped after almost every syllable, and moreover she spoke so softly that I had difficulty in hearing her, although my ear was almost touching her mouth. I took the key, pointed to the oratory, she nodded her assent; but then, realizing that I was going to lose her and feeling sure that her illness was a result either of mine or of all the trouble she had taken or the care she had lavished upon me, I began to cry and lament in a loud voice. I kissed her on the forehead, eyes, face and hands and begged her forgiveness, but her mind seemed to be elsewhere and she did not hear me. One of her hands rested on my face and stroked it. I think she could not see me any more, and perhaps even thought I had gone, for she called out:

'Sister Suzanne?'

'Here I am.'

'What is the time?'

'Half past eleven.'

'Half past eleven! Go and have some food; go and come straight back.'

The dinner bell rang and I had to leave her. When I reached the door she called me back. I went back and she made an effort to offer me her cheeks, which I kissed, she took my hand and held it tight as though she would not or could not let it go. 'And yet it must be,' she said as she did let go. 'It is God's will. Good-bye, Sister Suzanne. Give me my crucifix.' I put it in her hands and went away.

They were about to leave the table. I went up to the Superior, and in front of all the other nuns told her of the danger Sister Ursule was in and urged her to go and see for herself. 'Oh well,' she said, 'I suppose I'd better see her.' She went up with a few others, and I followed. They entered the cell; our poor sister was no more, she was lying on her bed fully dressed, with her head turned on to her pillow, mouth half open and eyes shut, and the crucifix was in her hands. The Superior looked coldly at her and said: 'She is dead. Who would have thought she was so near to her end? She was an excellent young woman: go and ring the bell for her and have her buried.'

I stayed alone by her bed. I cannot describe my grief, and yet I envied her fate. I bent over her, shed tears, kissed her again and again and then pulled the sheet up over her face, which was already beginning to change. Then I considered carrying out what she had asked me to do. So as not to be interrupted in the middle of this, I waited until everybody was in chapel, then I opened the oratory, removed the partition and found a fairly thick bundle of papers which I burned that very evening. That young woman had always been melancholy, and I have no recollection of seeing her smile except once during her illness.

So now I was alone in that convent and in the world, for I did not know a single person who would be interested in me. I had heard no more of the lawyer Manouri, and I presumed either that he had been discouraged by the difficulties or that he had been taken up with amusements and business, so that the offers he had made me were long forgotten, and I could not altogether blame him. My character tends to be indulgent, and I can forgive men anything except injustice, ingratitude and inhumanity. So I was making allowances for Monsieur Manouri as far as I could, and all those people who had shown so much persistence during my case, and to whom my case now seemed closed, and for you too, Sir. But at that moment our ecclesiastical overseers came and carried out a visitation in the convent.

They come in, go through the cells, question the nuns, demand an account of the temporal and spiritual administration, and according to the spirit in which they interpret their functions, they put any disorder right or make it worse. So I once again saw the good but stern Monsieur Hébert and his two young and sympathetic attendants. They apparently remembered the deplorable condition in which I had previously appeared before them, and their eyes shone with tears as their faces expressed affection and joy. Monsieur Hébert sat down and made me sit opposite him, his two companions stood behind his chair, looking at me closely. Monsieur Hébert said:

'Well Suzanne, and how are they treating you now?'

I answered: 'Sir, they forget I exist.'

'That's all to the good.'

'And it is all I could wish for too, but there is one important favour I would like to ask of you, and that is to summon the Mother Superior to come here.'

'And why?'

'Because if it should so happen that anybody complains to you about her, she will certainly fix the blame on me.'

'I understand, but all the same tell me what you know about her.'

'Sir, I beg you to have her summoned here so that she can hear for herself your questions and my answers.'

'Tell me all the same.'

'Sir, it will mean disaster for me.'

'No it won't, there's nothing to fear; from today on you cease to be under her authority, and before the week is out you will be transferred to Saint-Eutrope, near Arpajon. You have one good friend.'

'A good friend, Sir? I don't know of one.'

'Your lawyer.'

'Monsieur Manouri?'

'The same.'

'I didn't think he would still remember me.'

'He has seen your sisters, he has seen the Archbishop, the First President and all sorts of people known for their piety, he has arranged a dowry for you in the convent I have just mentioned, and you have only a short time left to stay here. Therefore if you know of any irregularity you can tell me about it without compromising yourself, and I order you to on holy obedience.'

'I don't know of any.'

'What, have they been careful to keep within bounds with you since you lost your case?'

'They believed, and were right in believing, that I had committed a sin by appealing against my vows, and they made me ask God's forgiveness.'

'But it is the manner in which this was done that I want to know.'

He shook his head and frowned as he said these words, and I knew that it was in my power to return to the Superior some of the disciplinary treatment she had dealt out to me, but that was not my object. Realizing that he would get nothing out of me, the Archdeacon left, recommending secrecy concerning what he had revealed about my transference to Sainte-Eutrope d'Arpajon.

While the worthy Hébert was walking alone in the corridor, his two companions came back and spoke to me very kindly and affectionately. I don't know who they are, but may God preserve in them this quality of loving kindness which is so rare in their position and which is so right in those whose function is to be recipients of men's weaknesses and to intercede on their behalf for the mercy of God. I thought Monsieur Hébert was busy consoling, questioning or reprimanding some other nun when he came back to my cell and said:

'How did you come to know Monsieur Manouri?'

'Through my lawsuit.'

'Who put you in touch with him?'

'Madame la Présidente.'

'You have had to confer with him often in the course of your affair?'

'No, Sir, I have seen very little of him.'

'Then how did you give him his instructions?'

'With a few memoranda in my own writing.'

'Have you copies of these memoranda?'

'No, Sir.'

'Who passed them on to him?'

'Madame la Présidente.'

'How did you know her?'

'I knew her through Sister Ursule, my friend, who was related to her.'

'Have you seen Monsieur Manouri since the loss of your case?'

'Once.'

'That isn't much. He hasn't written to you?'

'No, Sir.'

'Nor you to him?'

'No, Sir.'

'He will doubtless let you know what he has done for you. I order you not to see him in the parlour, and if he writes, either to you directly or indirectly, send me his letter unopened, you understand, unopened.'

'Yes, Sir, I will obey you.'

Whether Monsieur Hébert's distrust was directed at me or my benefactor, I was hurt.

Monsieur Manouri came to Longchamp that very evening, but I kept my word to the Archdeacon and refused to speak to him. The following day he wrote to me through his representative. I received his letter and sent it on unopened to Monsieur Hébert. That was on Tuesday, if I remember rightly. I was impatiently waiting for the result of the Archdeacon's promise and Monsieur Manouri's activities. Wednesday, Thursday and Friday went by with no news at all, and how long those days seemed! I was terrified that some hitch had occurred and upset everything. I was not getting back my freedom, but was changing prisons, and that was something. One thing that goes well raises our hopes for a second, which is perhaps the origin of the saying that *good things, like troubles, never come singly.*

I knew the companions I was leaving, and it was not difficult to imagine that I might be better off living with a different set of prisoners – whatever they were like they couldn't be more spiteful or ill-intentioned. On Saturday morning at about nine there was a great commotion in the house; it doesn't need much to turn the heads of a lot of nuns. They came and went, whispered; dormitory doors opened and shut; as you have already seen, these are the signals for convent upheavals. I was alone in my cell, my heart was beating fast. I listened at the door, looked out of my window, busied myself without knowing what I was doing, saying to myself with a thrill of joy: 'They are coming for me; in a minute I shan't be here any more.' And I was right.

Two unknown figures appeared. They were a nun and the portress from Arpajon, and they told me in a word why they had come. I rapturously seized the few treasures I possessed and threw them in a jumble into the portress's apron and she made them into a parcel. I did not ask to see the Mother Superior – Sister Ursule was no more and I had nobody to leave. I go down, after an inspection of what I am taking away the doors are opened, I get into a carriage and off I go.

The Archdeacon and his two young priests, Madame la Présidente and Monsieur Manouri had met in the Superior's room, where they were told of my departure. On the journey the nun told me about the establishment, and to each phrase of this eulogy the portress added as a refrain: 'It's the absolute truth!' She was honoured to be chosen to come for me and wanted to be my friend, and in consequence she confided a few secrets to me and gave me various bits of advice on how I should behave, advice apparently for her own benefit, for it could not have been for mine. I don't know whether you have seen the convent at Arpajon. It is a square building with one side facing the main road and the other the gardens and open country. Every window on the first floor had one, two or three nuns peeping out, and this circumstance alone revealed to me more about the sort of order that reigned in the house than everything the nun and her companion had told me. Apparently the carriage bringing us was well known, for in the twinkling of an eye all these veiled heads had vanished, and I reached the door of my new prison. The Mother Superior came out to meet me with arms outstretched, kissed me, took my hand and led me into the reception room, where some of the nuns had arrived before me, and others rushed in.

This Superior is called Madame***. I cannot resist my desire to describe her before going any further. She is short and quite plump, yet quick and lively in her movements, her head is never held straight on her shoulders, there is always something wrong with her clothes, her face is good-looking rather than plain, and her eyes, one of which, the right one, is higher and larger than the other, are full of fire and far-away looking. When she walks she swings her arms backwards and forwards. Should she want to speak, she opens her mouth before sorting out her ideas, so she tends to -um and -ah somewhat. Should she be sitting down she

wriggles on her chair as though something were bothering
her, forgetting all sense of decorum she lifts her wimple so
as to scratch, crosses her legs, asks you questions but does
not listen when you answer, says something to you, loses
the thread and stops short, has forgotten where she is, gets
annoyed and calls you a great silly, foolish, stupid if you
don't set her on the right track again; she is sometimes
familiar to the point of my-dearing you, and sometimes
haughty and imperious to the point of disdain; her moments of dignity are short, she is in turn compassionate and
hard, her ever-changing expression indicates the discon-
nectedness of her mind and all the instability of her character. And so order and disorder succeed each other in the
convent: there were days when everything was at sixes and
sevens, boarders mixed up with novices, novices with nuns,
and people ran in and out of each other's rooms, everybody
had tea, coffee, chocolate or liqueurs together and the
church services were rushed through with the most unseemly haste, and then in the middle of this tumult the
Superior's face would suddenly change, the bell tolled, everyone shut herself up and retired, and the deepest silence followed the din, the shouting and tumult, and you would
have thought everything had suddenly died. If at such a
time a nun should be in the slightest degree remiss, she
sends for her, treats her harshly, orders her to undress and
give herself twenty strokes with the scourge. The nun
obeys, takes off her clothes, takes up the scourge and chas-
tises herself, but scarcely has she given herself one or two
strokes than the Superior comes over all compassionate,
snatches the instrument of penitence away from her, bursts
into tears and says how dreadful it is for her to have to
punish anybody, kisses the nun on the forehead, eyes,
mouth and shoulders, caresses and flatters her: 'But what a
soft, white skin she has! such a lovely figure! lovely neck
and hair! Sister Sainte-Augustine, you really are silly to be
so bashful, slip off your chemise, I am a woman, dear, and
your Superior. Oh what a beautiful bosom! And so firm!
And could I let it be torn by spikes? No, no, nothing of the

kind...' She then kisses her again, helps her up, dresses her herself, saying all sorts of nice things to her, excuses her from office and sends her back to her cell. You are very ill at ease with women like that and never know what will please or displease them, what to avoid or do; nothing is stable, you are either served lavishly or dying of hunger, the running of the institution gets into a muddle, any remonstrances are taken the wrong way or else ignored. You are always too near or too far away from Superiors of this kind, there is no real distance or proportion; you pass from disgrace to favour and from favour to disgrace without knowing why. Let me give you one little thing as an example of the whole of her administration. Twice a year she would run round from cell to cell and have any bottles of spirits she found thrown out of the windows, and four days later she herself would send some more to most of the nuns. Such was the woman to whom I had made a solemn vow of obedience, for we transfer our vows from one convent to another.

So I went in with her, and she led me with her arm round my waist. Some refreshments were served: fruit, marzipan and preserves. The solemn Archdeacon began to sing my praises, but she interrupted him with: 'They were wrong, they were wrong, I know.' The solemn Archdeacon tried to go on but she interrupted him with: "However could they have sent her away? She is modesty and gentleness itself, and it seems she is extremely talented...' The solemn Archdeacon tried to take up the thread again, but she interrupted yet again and whispered into my ear: 'I simply dote on you, and when those pedants have gone I will get some of our sisters to come and you will sing us a little tune, won't you?' I suddenly wanted to giggle. The solemn Monsieur Hébert was a little put out, and his two companions smiled at his embarrassment and mine. But by then Monsieur Hébert recovered his usual character and way of behaving, and sharply ordered her to sit down and keep quiet. She sat down but was not at all comfortable, and wriggled in her seat, scratched her head, put right her veil where there was nothing wrong with it, yawned, and all the time the Archdeacon was holding forth very sensibly about the convent I had left and the unpleasantness I had gone through there, about the convent I was entering and the debt I owed those people who had been of assistance. At this I looked at Monsieur Manouri, who lowered his eyes. Thereafter the conversation became more general and the painful silence imposed upon the Superior came to an end. I went up to Monsieur Manouri and thanked him for the services he had rendered me. I was trembling and stammering and did not know what sort of gratitude to promise him. My confusion, embarrassment and emotion, for I was deeply touched, a mixture of tears and joy, in fact my whole demeanour spoke to him more clearly than I could have done. His answer was no more studied than my speech, and he was as deeply moved as I was. I don't know what he said to me, but I gathered that he felt he would be sufficiently rewarded to have softened the harshness of my lot, that he would look back upon what he had done with even more pleasure than myself, and that he was very sorry indeed that his profession, which kept him to the Palais de Justice in Paris, would not allow him to visit the cloister at Arpajon very often, but that he trusted that the Archdeacon and the Reverend Mother would permit him to inquire about my health and circumstances.

The Archdeacon did not hear all this, but the Superior chimed in: 'Sir, as often as you like; she will do whatever you wish. We shall try here to make up for the troubles she has had inflicted upon her...' Then she whispered to me: 'My child, have you been through a great deal? How could those creatures at Longchamp have dared to ill-treat you so? I have met your Superior, we were trained together at Port-Royal, and she was everybody else's pet abomination. We shall have time to see each other and you must tell me all about it, dear...' As she said this she took one of my hands and tapped it gently with hers. The young priests also paid me their respects. It was late, Monsieur Manouri took his leave and the Archdeacon and his companions went to see the lord of the manor of Arpajon, who had invited them, and so I was left alone with the Superior; but not for long, for all the nuns, all the novices and all the boarders trooped in, and in an instant I was surrounded by a hundred people. There were faces of all kinds and things of all sorts being said, and I didn't know whom to listen to or to answer, yet I could see that they were not displeased with my answers or with my person.

When this tiresome cross-examination had gone on for some time and their first curiosity had been satisfied, the crowd thinned and the Superior edged the rest to one side and herself came to see me installed in my cell. She did the honours, after her fashion, and as she showed me the oratory she said: 'This is where my dear little friend will say her prayers; I will see that a hassock is put on this step so that her little knees are not hurt. There is no holy water in this stoup – that Sister Dorothy always forgets something. Try this armchair and see if it suits you...'

And, still talking away, she sat me down, tilted my head against the back of the chair and kissed me on the forehead. Then she went to the window to make sure that the sashes went up and down easily, to my bed, where she drew the curtains across and back again to see if they closed properly. She examined the bedclothes: 'Yes, they are all right.' She took the bolster and plumped it up, saying: 'Dear little head will be nice and comfy on that; these sheets are not very fine, but they are the community ones; the mattresses are good...' This done she came over to me, kissed me and departed. While all this was going on I said to myself: 'Oh what a scatterbrained creature!' And I expected good and bad days.

I settled myself in to my cell, went to evening service and to supper and recreation afterwards. Some of the nuns made for me and other avoided me, the former counting on my influence with the Superior, the latter already disturbed by the favour she had shown me. These first moments were devoted to compliments on both sides, questions about the house I had left, soundings of my character, likes and dislikes, tastes and intelligence: you are felt all over, a little series of traps is set for you, from which they draw perfectly correct conclusions. For instance, somebody drops a word of gossip, and you are watched, somebody begins telling a story and they wait to see whether you ask for the rest or don't take it up; if you make some commonplace remark it is called delightful, although they know quite well it is nothing of the kind; you are praised or criticized on purpose, they try to delve into your most secret thoughts; you are questioned about what you read, offered sacred and profane books and note is taken of what you choose; you are urged to commit slight infringements of the rules, you are told secrets, odd words are dropped about the curious behaviour of the Superior. And everything is stored up and repeated. You are dropped and taken up again, you are sounded for your opinions on morals, piety, the outside world, religion, the monastic life, everything. From these repeated experiments there results an epithet which characterizes you, and it is attached like a surname to the name you bear. I was called Sainte-Suzanne the Reserved.

On the first evening I was visited by the Superior, who came to my formal undressing, and she herself took off my veil and wimple and arranged my hair for the night; in fact she undressed me. She said a hundred nice things to me and lavished on me a thousand caresses, which somewhat embarrassed me, why I don't know, for I did not understand quite what was happening and neither did she. And even now, when I come to think it over, what could we have understood? Nevertheless I did mention it to my confessor, who treated this familiarity, which seemed innocent to me then and still does, in a very serious tone and solemnly warned me not to lend myself to it any more. She kissed my neck, shoulders and arms, praised my figure and proportions and put me to bed, arranged the blankets on both sides, kissed me on the eyes, drew my curtains and went away. I forgot to mention that she presumed I would be tired and gave me permission to stay in bed as long as I liked.

I availed myself of this and had what I think was the best night I ever spent in a convent, though I had hardly ever been anywhere else. Next morning at about nine I heard a gentle tap on my door. I was still in bed, I answered and somebody came in. It was a nun who told me rather snappily that it was late and Reverend Mother was asking for me. I got up, dressed hastily and went.

'Good morning, my child,' she said. 'Have you had a good night? Here is some coffee that has been waiting for you this whole hour. I think it will be all right. Hurry up and have it and then we can talk...'

While saying this she was spreading a napkin on the table, putting another on me, pouring out the coffee and sugaring it. The other nuns did similar things in each other's rooms. While I was having my breakfast she told me about my companions, describing them according to her likes and dislikes, said lots of kind things, asked lots of questions about the establishment I had left, my parents, the unpleasantness I had been through, accorded praise or blame as she saw fit, and never heard out my answers. As I did not contradict her she was pleased with my intelligence, judgement and discretion. Meanwhile a nun appeared, and then another, then a third and a fourth and a fifth, and talk ranged over Mama's pet birds, one went on about Sister's little oddities, another about the funny little ways of those who were absent, and jollity prevailed. There was a spinet in one corner of the room and I nonchalantly touched it with my fingers, for as I was a newcomer to the place and knew none of the people they were joking about, this talk did not interest me much, nor would it have done so even had I known more about it. You need far too much wit to make a good teller of jokes, and in any case who is without his ridiculous side? While they were all laughing I played a few chords, and gradually I attracted attention. The Superior came over, and tapping me on the shoulder said: 'Come along, Sainte-Suzanne, entertain us. Play first, and then you can sing afterwards.' I did what she told me, and played one or two pieces I had at my fingers' ends, I improvised, then sang a few verses of Mondonville's setting of the Psalms.

'That's all very well,' said the Superior, 'but we have as much holiness as we want in church. We are by ourselves and these are all my friends and will also be yours, my dear. Sing us something more amusing.'

Some of the nuns said: 'But that may be all she knows; she is tired after her journey and we must spare her. That is quite enough for once.'

'No, no,' said the Superior, 'she accompanies herself beautifully, she has the loveliest voice in the world [it is true that my voice is far from ugly, but it is sweet and flexible rather than powerful or wide in range], and I won't let her off until she has sung something else.'

I was a little put out by what the nuns had said, and so I answered the Superior that they were no longer interested.

'But I still am.'

I suspected that this would be the answer. So I sang a delicate little air and they all clapped, praised me, embraced and caressed me and asked for another – deceitful little endearments prompted by the Superior's reaction, for there was hardly one of them who would not have deprived me of my voice and broken my fingers if she had been able to. Women who had not perhaps listened to a note of music in their lives took it into their heads to give vent to opinions as ridiculous as they were offensive about my singing, but these did not work with the Superior.

'That will do,' she told them. 'She plays and sings like an angel, and I want her to come here every day. I could play a little myself years ago, and I want her to help me to recover my skill.'

'Oh Madame,' I said, 'when you have once known how you don't forget it all.'

'Very well, let me take your place.'

She improvised and played weird, strange things as disconnected as her ideas, but in spite of all the defects in her execution, I saw that she had infinitely more agile fingers than mine. I told her so, for I enjoy praising people, and have seldom lost a chance of doing so if it is deserved, for it is such a nice thing to do! The nuns vanished one after another and I was left almost alone with the Superior, talking about music. She was seated and I standing; she took my hands, pressed them and said: 'But as well as playing so well, she has the prettiest fingers in the world. Look, Sister Thérèse...' Sister Thérsèe lowered her eyes, blushed and stammered, but whether I had pretty fingers or not, whether the Superior was right or wrong to remark on them, what had it to do with this nun? The Superior put her arm round my waist and decided that I had a lovely figure. By now she had drawn me close and sat me on her knee; she tilted my face upwards with her hand and made me look straight at her. She praised my eyes, mouth, cheeks, complexion, but I made no answer but passively let myself be caressed. Sister Thérèse was unsettled, restless and walked up and down, touching everything needlessly, not knowing what to do with herself, looking out of the window, thinking she heard someone knocking at the door. So the Superior said: 'Sister Thérèse, you can go if you are bored.'

'Reverend Mother, I am not bored.'

'I have thousands of things to ask this girl.'

'I can well believe it.'

'I want to know all her story, for how can I make up for the distress that has been inflicted upon her if I don't know about it? I want her to tell me without any omissions. I am sure it will rend my heart and make me cry, but no matter. Sainte-Suzanne, when shall I know everything?'

'When you order me to tell you, Reverend Mother.'

'I would beg you to do it now if we had the time. What time is it?'

Sister Thérèse answered: 'Madame, it is five o'clock and the bell is going to ring for Vespers.'

'Let her start all the same.'

'But, Madame, you had promised me a moment of consolation before Vespers. I have disquieting thoughts and would like to open my heart to dearest Mother. If I go to service without that I shall not be able to pray and my mind will wander.'

'No, no,' said the Superior, 'you are so silly with these ideas of yours. I wager I know what it is, and we'll talk about it tomorrow.'

'Ah, dear Mother,' said Sister Thérèse, throwing herself at the Superior's feet and bursting into tears, 'let it be now!'

'Madame,' I said, getting up from the Superior's knee, where I still was, 'grant Sister what she is asking. Don't let her distress go on any longer. I am going now, and I shall always have time to satisfy the interest you are good enough to take in me, and when you have heard Sister Thérèse she won't suffer any more...'

I made as if to go towards the door, but the Superior held me with one hand while Thérèse, on her knees, had seized the other and was kissing it and weeping. The Superior said:

'Really, Sainte-Thérèse, your anxieties are very ill-timed; I have already told you that I don't like it, it upsets me and I don't want to be upset.'

'I know, but I am not mistress of my own feelings. I would like to be, but I can't.'

But by now I had gone and left the young nun with the Superior. I could not help watching her in church, and she was still disconsolate and miserable. Our eyes met several times, and I felt that she found it hard to bear my scrutiny. As for the Superior, she had dozed off in her stall.

The service was dispatched in the twinkling of an eye. The choir did not seem to me to be the part of the establishment in which they took the greatest pleasure. Everybody rushed out with the speed and babble of a flock of birds escaping from their cage, and the sisters wandered off into each other's rooms, running, laughing and chattering. The Superior shut herself up in her cell and Sister Thérèse paused on the threshold of hers, watching me as though curious to know what I was going to do. I went into my own room and Sister Thérèse's door was only shut some time later, and then very softly. It occurred to me that this girl was jealous of me and was afraid I would steal the place she occupied in the good graces and favour of the Superior. I watched her for several days, and when I felt my suspicions reasonably endorsed by her little tempers, childish alarms, determination to follow me about, examine me, come between the Superior and me, interrupt our conversations, belittle my qualities and show up my defects, but still more by her pallor, sadness, tears and deterioration in health and even mind, I went to see her and said: 'Dear friend, what is the matter with you?'

She made no answer, for my visit had caught her unawares and embarrassed her, and she didn't know what to say or do.

'You are doing me less than justice; own up and say that you are afraid I shall take advantage of the liking Reverend Mother has developed for me and oust you from her affections. Rest assured, that is not in my character, and if I were ever fortunate enough to have any influence over her mind...'

'You will have as much as you like because she loves you and is doing for you exactly what she did for me in the early stages.'

'Well then, you can be sure I shall never use the confidence she places in me except to make her cherish you more.'

'But will that depend on you?'

'Why not?'

Instead of replying she fell on my neck and sighed as she said: 'It isn't your fault, I know that perfectly well and tell myself so every minute, but promise me...'

'What do you want me to promise?'

'That...'

'Say it. I will do anything that depends on me.'

She hesitated, put her hands over her eyes and said so softly that I could hardly hear: '...that you will see her as seldom as you can.'

This seemed such a strange request that I couldn't help replying: 'How does it affect you whether I see our Superior often or not? I don't mind in the least if you see her all the time. You shouldn't mind any the more if I do the same. Isn't it enough for me to protest that I shall never damage you or anybody else in her eyes?'

She made no reply except in these agonized words as she tore herself away from me and hurled herself on to her bed: 'I am a lost soul!'

'A lost soul! Why? You must think me the most evil creature in the world.'

We were at that point when the Superior came in. She had gone to my cell and not found me there, then had rushed all over most of the house in vain, for it never entered her head that I was with Sister Sainte-Thérèse. When she had found this out from those she had sent to look for me, she came with all speed. There was something odd about her face and eyes, but then she was so seldom all in one piece! Sainte-Thérèse was sitting silent on her bed, I was standing. I said: 'Dear Reverend Mother, I beg pardon for coming here without your permission.'

'It would certainly have been better to ask for it.'

'But this poor sister filled me with pity, and I saw that she was in distress.'

'What about?'

'Shall I tell you? But why shouldn't I? It is a sign of delicacy which does great honour to her spirit and so clearly shows her attachment to you. The kindnesses you have shown me have given her affection cause for alarm, and she feared I might gain preference over her in your heart. This feeling of jealousy, quite right and proper, of course, and so natural and flattering for you, dear Reverend Mother, had become a torture to our sister, I thought, and I was comforting her.'

Having heard me out the Superior adopted a severe and majestic air and said:

'Sister Thérèse, I have been very fond of you and I still am. I have nothing against you and you will have nothing to complain of from me, but I cannot put up with these exclusive claims. If you have any fear of killing what affection I have left for you, you must give them up, and if you remember what happened to Sister Agathe ...' She then turned to me and said: 'That is the tall dark one you see in the choir opposite me' (I went about so little and I had been such a short time at the convent and was so new to it that I did not yet know the names of all my companions.) She went on: 'I loved her, and then when Sister Thérèse came here I began to be fond of her too. She had just the same emotions and was just as silly; I warned her but she did not mend her ways, and I was obliged to resort to stronger measures which went on far too long and which are quite out of keeping with my character; for everybody will tell you that I am good-natured and never use punishments except against my will...'

Then she said to Sainte-Thérèse: 'My child, I don't want to be upset, as I have told you already. You know me; don't make me act out of character.' Then she put one hand on my shoulder and said: 'Come along, Sainte-Suzanne, take me back.'

We left. Sister Thérèse made as if to follow us, but looking back casually over my shoulder the Superior said harshly: 'Go back to your cell and don't leave it until I give permission.' She did so, and slammed the door, giving vent to some observations which made the Superior flinch, I don't know why, for they made no sense to me, but seeing her anger I said: 'Dear Reverend Mother, if you have any kind feelings for me, forgive Sister Thérèse. She is very upset and doesn't know what she is saying or doing.'

'Forgive her! Gladly, but what will you give me?'

'Oh, Reverend Mother, could I be fortunate enough to possess something you would like and which would soften your heart?'

She lowered her eyes, blushed and sighed – really just like a lover. Leaning nonchalantly against me, as though she felt faint, she said: 'Give me your forehead to kiss,' I bent down and she kissed my forehead. From that time on as soon as a nun had committed some offence I interceded for her and was sure to earn her forgiveness by granting some innocent favour: always a kiss on the forehead or neck,

eyes, cheeks, mouth, hands, bosom or arms, but most often
on the mouth, for she thought I had sweet breath, white
teeth and fresh ruby lips.

I would have been beautiful indeed had I deserved a frac-
tion of the eulogies she bestowed: if it was my forehead, it
was white, smooth and beautifully shaped; if my eyes, they
were sparkling; if my cheeks, they were pink and soft; if my
hands, they were tiny and dimpled; if my bosom, it was firm
as a statue and admirably formed; if my arms, it was impossible to have them better turned and rounded; if my
neck, not one of the sisters had a better one and more ex-
quisitely unusual in its beauty – and I don't know all she did
say! There was certainly an element of truth in her praises,
and I discounted a good deal, but not all. Sometimes, looking me up and down with a delight I had never seen in any
woman, she would say: 'No, it is the greatest blessing that
God has called her into the cloister, for in the world, with
that face, she would have damned as many men as she set
eyes on, and been damned along with them. All that God
does, He does well.'

By this time we were nearing her cell, and I was preparing to leave her, but she held my hand and said: 'It is too
late to begin your story of Sainte-Marie and Longchamp.
But do come in, and you can give me a little music lesson.'

I followed her in. In an instant she had opened the keyboard, produced a book, moved up a chair, for she was
quick in her movements. I sat down. Thinking I might be
chilly she removed a cushion from the chairs, which she put
in front of me and bent down, took my feet and placed
them on the cushion. Then I played some pieces of Coup-
erin, Rameau and Scarlatti, during which she lifted a corner
of my collar and rested her hand on my bare shoulder, with
the tips of her fingers touching my breast. She was sighing
and seemed oppressed, breathing heavily. The hand on my
shoulder pressed hard at first but then ceased pressing at
all, as though all strength and life had gone out of her and
her head fell on to mine. Truly that hare-brained woman
was incredibly sensitive and had the most exquisite taste

for music, for I have never known anybody on whom it had such an extraordinary effect.

Thus we were enjoying ourselves in a manner as simple as it was pleasant, when suddenly the door was flung open. I was frightened, and so was the Superior; it was that crazy Sainte-Thérèse, her clothes in disarray, her eyes wild. She examined us both with the strangest attention, her lips trembled and she could not speak. Eventually she recovered herself and fell at the feet of the Superior; I joined her in intercession and once again obtained her pardon, but the Superior pointed out in the firmest way that this would be the last time, at any rate for offences of this kind, and we both left.

On the way back to our cells I said· 'Dear Sister, do be careful, you will upset Reverend Mother. I won't abandon you, but you will exhaust what little influence I may have with her, and I shall be terribly disappointed not to be able to do anything again for you or anybody else. Well, what do you think?'

No answer.

'What have you got to fear from me?'

No answer.

'Can't Reverend Mother love us both equally?'

'No, no,' she angrily replied, 'that is impossible. Soon she will loathe me and I shall die of grief. Oh, why did you come here? You won't be happy here for long, I can tell you, and I shall be wretched for ever.'

'But,' I said, 'I know it is a great misfortune to have lost the Superior's goodwill, but I know a worse one, and that is to have deserved to. You have nothing to reproach yourself with.'

'Oh, would to God that were true!'

'If you secretly blame yourself for some sin, you must put it right, and the best way is to bear the penalty with patience.'

'I simply couldn't, I couldn't. And then, what right has she to punish me?'

'She, Sister Thérèse, she! Can you talk like that about a

Superior? That is very wrong and you are forgetting yourself. I am sure that that is a much more serious offence than
anything you are accusing yourself of.'

'Oh, would to God!' she repeated, 'would to God!' And
we parted, she to go and fret in her cell and I to meditate in
mine about the strangeness of women's mentality.

There you have the effect of segregation. Man is born for
life in society; separate him, isolate him, and his ideas will
go to pieces, his character will go sour, a hundred ridiculous
affections will spring up in his heart, extravagant notions
will take root in his mind like tares in the wilderness. Put a
man in a forest and he will turn into a wild beast, but in a
cloister, where a feeling of duress combines with that of
servitude, it is worse still. There is a way out of a forest,
there is none out of a cloister; a man is free in the forest but
he is a slave in the cloister. It may well be that greater
strength of character is needed for standing up to solitude
than to poverty, for if poverty degrades us segregation de-
praves. Is it less bad to live in abjectness than in folly? I
would not dare to decide, but one must avoid both.

I could see the affection the Superior had conceived for
me growing from day to day. I was always in her cell or she
in mine; for the slightest indisposition she prescribed the
sick-room for me, excused me from offices, sent me to bed
early or forbade early morning prayers. In choir, refectory
or recreation she contrived to show her friendship; in choir,
if there was a verse containing some affectionate or tender
sentiment, she sang it to me or looked at me if it was sung
by another; in the refectory she always sent me part of
anything delicious that was served to her; in recreation she
would put her arm round my waist and say the sweetest
and kindest things; nobody gave her a present that I did
not share in: chocolate, sugar, coffee, liqueurs, snuff, linen,
handkerchiefs, whatever it was. She stripped her own cell of
pictures, china, furniture and a host of pleasant and useful
things so as to embellish mine, and I could scarcely leave
my room for a moment without finding on my return that
it had been enriched with gifts. Then I would go and thank

her, and that gave her indescribable pleasure, and she kissed me and hugged me, sat me on her knee, told me all the most confidential secrets of the convent and promised herself a life a thousand times happier than she would have had in the world outside, provided that I loved her. Then she would stop, look at me with eyes of love and say: 'Sister Suzanne, do you love me?'

'How could I fail to love you? I would have to be the very soul of ingratitude.'

'That is true.'

'You are so kind.'

'So fond of you . . .'

As she said these words she lowered her eyes and the hand round me tightened still more, and the one on my knee increased its pressure. She pulled me down to her, my face was against hers, she sighed and fell back on her chair trembling. It was as though she had some secret to tell me but dared not, and she shed tears and then said: 'Ah Sister Suzanne, you don't love me!'

'I don't love you, dear Mother?'

'No.'

'Tell me what I must do to prove it to you.'

'That you will have to guess.'

'I am trying, but I cannot think of anything.'

By now she had raised her collar and put one of my hands on her bosom. She fell silent, and so did I. She seemed to be experiencing the most exquisite pleasure. She invited me to kiss her forehead, cheeks, eyes and mouth, and I obeyed. I don't think there was any harm in that, but her pleasure increased, and as I was only too glad to add to her happiness in any innocent way, I kissed her again on forehead, cheeks, eyes and lips. The hand she had rested on my knee wandered all over my clothing from my feet to my girdle, pressing here and there, and she gasped as she urged me in a strange, low voice to redouble my caresses, which I did. Eventually a moment came, whether of pleasure or of pain I cannot say, when she went as pale as death, closed her eyes, and her whole body tautened violently, her lips were first pressed together and moistened with a sort of foam, then they parted and she seemed to expire with a deep sigh. I jumped up, thinking she had fainted, and was about to go and call for help. She half opened her eyes and said in a failing voice: 'You innocent girl! it isn't anything. What are you doing? Stop...' I looked at her, wild-eyed and uncertain whether I should stay or go. She opened her eyes again; she had lost her power of speech, and made signs that I should come back and sit on her lap again. I don't know what was going on inside me, I was afraid, my heart was thumping and I breathed with difficulty, I was upset, oppressed, shocked and frightened, my strength seemed to have left me and I was about to swoon. And yet I cannot say it was pain I was feeling. I went over to her and she once again motioned me to sit on her lap, which I did; she was half dead and I felt as though I were dying myself. We remained in that peculiar state for some time. If a nun had come upon us then she would certainly have been scared and would have imagined either that we had fainted or gone to sleep. However, the good Superior, for it is impossible to be so sensitive and not good, seemed to be recovering. She was still lying back in her chair and her eyes were still closed, but her face was lit up with the loveliest colour. She took one of my hands and kissed it, while I said to her: 'Dear Mother, you did give me a fright!' She smiled sweetly without opening her eyes. 'But haven't you been ill?'

'No.'

'I thought you were.'

'What innocence! ah, dear innocent child! How she appeals to me!'

As she said these words she sat up straight in her chair, threw her arms round me and kissed me hard on both cheeks, then said: 'How old are you?'

'Not quite twenty.'

'I can't believe it.'

'Dear Mother, nothing is truer.'

'I want to know the whole story of your life. Will you tell me?'

'Yes, dear Mother.'

'Everything?'

'Everything.'

'But somebody might come. Let us sit at the keyboard, and you will be giving me a lesson.'

We did so but, I don't know why, my hands shook and the page seemed just a lot of muddled notes and I simply could not play. I told her so and she began to laugh and took my place, but it was still worse, for she could hardly hold out her arms.

'My dear child,' she said, 'I can see that you are in no fit state to teach me, nor I to learn. I am rather tired, and must have some rest, so good-bye. Tomorrow, and no later, I want to know everything that has gone on in that dear little soul of yours; good-bye...'

At other times when I left she came with me to her door and watched me all the way down the corridor as far as mine, blew a kiss at me and only went into her room when I had gone into mine, but on this occasion she hardly rose, and it was as much as she could do to get to the armchair by her bed, where she sat down, laid her head upon her pillow, blew me a kiss with her hands and closed her eyes as I took myself off.

My cell was almost opposite that of Sainte-Thérèse, her door was open and she was watching for me. She stopped me and said:

'Oh, Sainte-Suzanne, you have come from our Mother's?'

'Yes.'

'Did you stay there long?'

'As long as she wanted me to.'

'That is not what you promised me.'

'I didn't promise you anything.'

'Would you dare tell me what you did there?'

Although I had nothing to reproach myself with I will admit, Sir, that her question embarrassed me. She saw it did, and insisted on an answer, so I replied:

'Dear Sister, you may not believe me, but you would believe our dear Mother, and I shall ask her to tell you.'

'My dear Sainte-Suzanne,' she cut in quickly, 'don't do that. You don't want to make my life a misery; she would never forgive me. You don't know what she is, she is capable of passing from the greatest tenderness to ferocity. I don't know what would happen to me. Promise to say nothing to her.'

'You mean that?'

'I beg of you on my knees. I am desperate. I see that I must make up my mind, and I will. Promise me you'll say nothing to her.'

I helped her to her feet and gave her my word; she relied on it and she was right. We retired to our cells, she to hers and I to mine.

Back in my own room I could not concentrate, I wanted to pray but could not; I tried to find something to do and began one task and gave it up for another, and that for yet another; my hands stopped of their own accord and I was so to speak stupid – I had never experienced anything like it. My eyes closed in spite of me and I fell into a little doze, although I never usually sleep in the daytime. When I woke up I questioned myself about what had passed between the Superior and me and examined my conscience. After a further examination I thought I could glimpse an answer, but they were such vague, crazy, ridiculous notions that I put them out of my mind. The result of my reflections was that it was probably an affliction to which she was subject, then another thought came, that perhaps the malady was catching, and that Sainte-Thérèse had caught it and I should too.

On the following day, after Matins, our Superior said to me: 'Sainte-Suzanne, today I hope to know everything that has happened to you. Come along.'

I went. She made me sit in her own armchair by her bed, while she sat on a slightly lower chair, so that I dominated her a little, for I am taller and was a bit higher as well. She was so near me that my knees were interlocked with hers, and she leaned on her bed. After a moment's pause I said:

'Although I am so young I have been through a great

deal of trouble. I shall soon have been in this world for twenty years, and it has been twenty years of suffering. I don't know whether I shall be able to tell you everything or whether you will have the heart to listen to it: family troubles, troubles in the convent of Sainte-Marie, troubles in the convent of Longchamp, troubles everywhere. Dear Mother, where do you want me to begin?'

'With the first.'

'But, dear Mother, it will be very long and very depressing, and I don't want to make you miserable for so long.'

'Don't be afraid, I love a good cry, and to be shedding tears is a delicious state for a sensitive soul. You must enjoy weeping too – you will wipe away my tears and I yours, and perhaps we shall be happy in the middle of the tale of your sufferings, and who knows where our emotion may lead us?' As she said these last words she looked at me from top to toe with eyes already wet with tears, took me by both hands and came even nearer until we were touching each other.

'Tell me, my child. I am ready and I feel in the most pressing mood for emotion, indeed I don't think I have ever in my life had a day more full of sympathy and affection...'

So I began my story more or less as I have been writing it to you. I cannot describe the effect it produced upon her, the sighs she heaved, the tears she shed, her expressions of indignation against my cruel parents, the horrible women at Sainte-Marie and those at Longchamp. I should be sorry if the smallest part of the ills she wished for them ever befell them, for I would not have wanted to tear a single hair out of the head of my most cruel enemy. Now and again she stopped me, stood up, walked about, then resumed her place, or she would raise her hands and eyes to heaven and then bury her head in my lap. When I told her about the scene in the dungeon and that of my exorcism and my public confession she almost shouted aloud, and when I ended my tale and stopped speaking she remained for some time bent over her bed with her head buried in

the coverlet and arms stretched out above her head. I said:
'Dear Mother, do forgive me for all the distress I have given
you, but I did warn you and you insisted on it.' But she only
answered with these words:

'What wicked creatures! Horrible creatures! Only in
convents can humanity sink so low. When hatred allies itself to habitual ill temper you don't know how far things
can go. Fortunately I am a kind woman and I love all my
nuns, and they have taken on something of my character,
some more and some less, but they all love each other. But
how did that poor health of yours manage to stand up to
such torments? How comes it that all these fragile limbs
were not broken? And that delicate mechanism destroyed?
Why was the lustre of those eyes not dimmed for ever by
tears? What cruel women! Fancy crushing those arms with
ropes!' And she took my arms and kissed them. 'Drowning
those eyes in tears!' And she kissed them. 'Drawing groans
and wailing from that mouth!' She kissed that too. 'Condemning that charming, serene face to be constantly
clouded by sadness!' She kissed it. 'Making the roses of
those cheeks wither!' She stroked them with her hand and
kissed them. 'Robbing that head of its beauty! tearing out
that hair! loading that brow with sorrow!' She kissed my
head, brow, hair. 'Fancy daring to put a rope round that
neck and tearing those shoulders with sharp points!' She
pushed aside my collar and coif, opened the top of my dress
and my hair fell loose over my bare shoulders; my breast
was half uncovered and her kisses spread over my neck,
bare shoulders and half-naked breast.

The trembling that began to come over her, the confusion of her speech, the uncontrolled movements of her
eyes and hands, her knee pressing between mine, the ardour
of her embraces and the tightness of her arms as she held
me, all showed me that her malady was about to come over
her again. I don't know what was going on inside me, but I
was seized with panic, and my own trembling and faintness
justified the suspicion I had had that her trouble was contagious.

I said: 'Dear Mother, look what state you have put me in! If anybody were to come...'

'Stay here, stay here,' she said in a failing voice, 'nobody is going to come.'

But I struggled to get up and free myself from her, saying: 'Dear Mother, do be careful, your illness is coming on. Let me go away...'

I wanted to get away, I really did, but could not. I had no strength left and my legs were giving way. She was sitting and I standing up, she pulled me and I was afraid of falling on top of her and hurting her, so I sat on the edge of her bed and said:

'I don't know what's the matter with me. I feel faint.'

'So do I, but relax a moment and it will pass. It won't be anything.'

And indeed my Superior regained her composure, and so did I, but we were both exhausted. I had my head on her pillow and she rested hers on one of my knees, with her forehead on one of my hands. We remained in that state for some minutes. I wasn't thinking of anything, nor could I, for my weak state took up the whole of my attention. We said nothing, but the Superior was the first to break the silence: 'Suzanne, from what you have told me of her I have got the impression that you were very attached to your first Superior.'

'Very.'

'She did not love you any more than I do, but you loved her more ... You have no answer?'

'I was unhappy, and she comforted me in my distress.'

'But where does your distaste for the religious life come from? Suzanne, you haven't told me everything.'

'Excuse me, Madame, I have.'

'What! it's not possible, nice as you are – for, my dear child, you are very nice, and you don't realize yourself how nice you are – that nobody has told you so.'

'Yes, I have been told so.'

'And you didn't dislike the man who told you?'

'No.'

'You didn't feel any liking for him?'

'None whatever.'

'What, hasn't your heart ever felt anything?'

'No, nothing.'

'So it isn't some passion, secret or disapproved of by your parents, which turned you against convents? Let me into the secret, I am indulgent.'

'Dear Mother, I have no secret of that kind to confide in you.'

'Then once again, where does your distaste for the religious life come from?'

'From the life itself. I hate its duties, occupations, seclusion, constraint, and I feel I am called to do something else.'

'But what makes you feel like that?'

'The boredom that overwhelms me; I am bored.'

'Even here?'

'Yes, dear Mother, even here, in spite of all your kindness to me.'

'But do you feel any urges or desires within yourself?'

'No, none.'

'So it seems. It looks to me as though you have a very equable temperament.'

'Fairly.'

'Even frigid.'

'I couldn't say.'

'You don't know the world outside?'

'Very little.'

'Then what attraction can it have for you?'

'That isn't very clear to me, but there must be some.'

'Is it your freedom that you miss?'

'Yes it is that, and perhaps many other things.'

'And what are those other things? My dear, open your heart to me; would you like to be married?'

'I would prefer that to being what I am, for certain.'

'Why?'

'I don't know.'

'You don't know? Now tell me, what impression does a man's presence make on you?'

'None, but if he is intelligent and speaks well I enjoy listening to him, and if he has a handsome face, I notice it.'

'And your heart is untouched?'

'So far it has felt no emotion.'

'What! When they have looked into your eyes with ardour, haven't you felt –?'

'Sometimes I have felt embarrassed, and that made me drop my eyes.'

'But no stirring of emotion?'

'None.'

'Your senses didn't have anything to say to you?'

'I don't know what the language of the senses is.'

'And yet they do have a language.'

'That may well be.'

'But you don't know it?'

'Not at all.'

'What! You ... It is a very tender language. Wouldn't you like to learn it?'

'No, dear Mother, what use would it be to me?'

'It would drive away your boredom.'

'It might add to it, though. And then, what does this language of the senses mean, if it has no object?'

'When we talk it is always to somebody, and that is better, surely, than talking to oneself, although that is not altogether without pleasure.'

'I don't follow any of this.'

'If you wished, my dear child, I would make myself clearer.'

'No, dear Mother, no. I know nothing, and I would rather know nothing than acquire knowledge which might make me unhappier than I am now. I have no desires, and I don't want to discover any I couldn't satisfy.'

'But why couldn't you?'

'How could I?'

'As I do.'

'As you do! But there is nobody in this place.'

'I am here, my dear, and so are you.'

'Well, what am I to you, and you to me?'

'How innocent she is!'

'Oh yes, I am, it is true, dear Mother, and I would rather die than cease to be so.'

I don't know in what way these last words were unpleasant to her, but they made her change her expression at once. She became serious and embarrassed, and her hand, which she had rested on one of my knees, first stopped its pressure and then was moved away. She kept her eyes lowered.

I said: 'Dear Mother, what have I done? Has something escaped me which has upset you? Forgive me. I am using the freedom you have given me, and nothing I have to say to you is in any way studied, and besides, if I were to think it out I wouldn't put it any differently and might not do it as well. The things we are discussing are so novel to me! Forgive me...'

So saying, I threw my arms round her neck and laid my head on her shoulder. She put her arms round me and held me very tenderly. For a few minutes we remained thus, and then, recovering her calmly affectionate manner, she said:

'Suzanne, do you sleep well?'

'Very well, especially just recently.'

'Do you go to sleep at once?'

'Most often.'

'But when you don't drop off at once what do you think about?'

'My past life, the life I have still to come, or I pray to God, or I weep – all sorts of things.'

'And in the morning when you wake up early?'

'I get up.'

'At once?'

'At once.'

'You don't like just dreaming?'

'No.'

'Enjoying the lovely warmth of the bed?'

'No.'

'Never...?'

She paused at that word, and she was right, for what she was about to ask me was not seemly, and perhaps I shall be even more unseemly if I repeat it, but I have resolved to keep nothing back. 'You have never been tempted to consider with some self-satisfaction how beautiful you are?'

'No, dear Mother. I don't know whether I am as beautiful as you say, but even if I were, one is beautiful for others, and not for oneself.'

'It has never occurred to you to run your hands over that lovely bosom, those legs, that body, that firm, soft, white flesh of yours?'

'Oh no, that is sinful, and if such a thing had happened to me I don't know how I could ever have mentioned it in my confession...'

I don't know what else we said to each other, but then she was told she was wanted in the parlour. I thought the arrival of this visitor vexed her and she would have preferred to go on talking to me, although what we were saying was hardly worth regretting. However, we separated.

The community had never been happier than since I had joined it. The Superior seemed to have lost her moody character and they said I had steadied her. She even granted in my honour several recreation days and what are called feasts, that is to say days when the fare is a little better than usual, offices briefer and all the time between given over to recreation. But that happy time was soon to come to an end for the others as well as for me.

The scene I have just described was followed by many others which I pass over. Here is the sequel to it.

The Superior began to give way to restlessness and she lost her gaiety, freshness and sleep. On the following night, when everybody was asleep and the whole house silent, she rose and wandered about the corridors for some time, finally coming to my cell. I am a light sleeper, and I thought I recognized her step. She stopped still. Apparently letting her head fall forward against my door she made enough noise to wake me even if I had been asleep. I made not a sound; I thought I heard a voice lamenting, somebody sighing, and it made me shudder, and then I made up my mind to say *Ave*. Instead of answering she tiptoed away, but came back a little later, and the moanings and sighings began again. Once again I cried *Ave*, and she went away a second time. I felt reassured and went to sleep. While I was asleep somebody came in and sat by my bed, the curtains were drawn aside and a little candle was held so as to light up my face while the person holding it watched me sleeping. Anyhow, that is what I gathered from her attitude when I opened my eyes, and the person was the Mother Superior.

I sat up at once, and seeing how frightened I was she said: 'Suzanne, don't be afraid, it's me.' I let my head fall back on the pillow and said: 'Dear Mother, what are you doing here at this hour of night? What has made you come? Why aren't you asleep?'

'I can't sleep and I shan't be able to for a long time. I am tormented by bad dreams, hardly do I close my eyes before the agonies you have suffered haunt my imagination. I can see you in the clutches of those inhuman creatures, your hair all over your face and your feet bleeding, torch in hand and a rope round your neck. I am convinced they are about to take your life, and I start and tremble and all my body breaks into a cold sweat. I want to rush to your rescue, I scream and wake up, then wait in vain for sleep to come back to me. This is what has happened to me tonight, and I feared that heaven was warning me of some disaster to my friend, so I got up, came to your door and listened. I had the impression that you were not asleep, you called out and I went away. I came back again and again you spoke. Yet again I went away, but came back for the third time, and thinking you were asleep I came in. I have been here beside you for some time now, afraid of waking you up. At first I hesitated about pulling back your curtains, and wanted to go away for fear of upsetting your rest, but I could not resist a desire to see whether my beloved Suzanne was well, so I looked at you. How beautiful you are to look at, even when asleep!'

'Dear Mother, how kind you are!'

'I am frozen, but now I know I have nothing to fear for you, my dear child, and so perhaps I shall sleep. Give me your hand.'

I did so.

'How gentle your pulse is! and regular! Nothing upsets it.'

'I sleep pretty soundly.'

'How lucky you are!'

'Dear Mother, you will get colder still.'

'Yes, you are right. Good-bye, my dear, good-bye. I am going now.'

But she did not go; she stayed there looking at me, and a tear fell from each of her eyes. 'Dear Mother,' I said, 'what is the matter? You're crying. How sorry I am to have told you about my troubles!' Thereupon she shut my door, blew out the candle and fell upon me. She lay beside me, outside my coverlet, holding me in her arms, her face was pressed to mine and her tears moistened my cheeks, she sighed and gasped out plaintively: 'Dearest friend, take pity on me!'

'Dear Mother, what is the matter? Are you ill? What can I do for you?'

'I am shaking and shivering, and a terrible chill is coming over me.'

'Would you like me to get up and give you my bed?'

'No, there is no need for you to get up; just turn back the cover a little so that I can get near you, warm myself and be healed.'

'But, dear Mother, that is forbidden. What would they say if it were known? I have seen nuns given penance for far less serious things. It happened in the convent of Sainte-Marie that a nun went into another's cell at night, for they were great friends, and I can't tell you how badly it was thought of. My confessor has sometimes asked me if anybody has ever suggested coming to sleep with me, and solemnly warned me not to allow it. I have even mentioned the caresses you have given me, which I thought quite innocent, but he doesn't think so. I don't know why I have forgotten his advice, for I had made up my mind to speak to you about it.'

'My dear,' she said, 'the whole place is asleep around us, and nobody will know anything. I am the one who rewards and punishes here, and whatever your confessor may say I cannot see what harm there is for one friend to take into her bed another friend who is very distressed and has come in the night in spite of the freezing weather to make sure her dear one isn't in any danger. Suzanne, haven't you ever shared the same bed at home with your sisters?'

'No, never.'

'But if there had been occasion wouldn't you have done so without hesitation? If your sister had been very frightened and was freezing cold, and had come and asked for a place beside you, would you have refused?'

'No, I don't think so.'

'And am I not your dear Mother?'

'Yes you are. But it is forbidden.'

'My dear, I forbid it in others, but I allow it to you, and am asking you to do so. Just let me warm myself a minute and then I'll go. Give me your hand.' I did so. 'Feel me, touch me and see for yourself. I am all shivering and stone cold.' And it was true. 'Oh, poor Reverend Mother,' I said, 'you will be ill. Just a moment, I will move over to one side and you can put yourself in the warm place.' I moved over to the side, lifted the coverlet and she came into my place. Oh, how upset she was! She was shaking in every limb, she wanted to talk to me and come nearer, but could neither say a word nor move. She whispered: 'Suzanne, my dear, come a bit nearer.' She held out her arms, but I had my back to her; she took me gently and pulled me towards her, passed her right arm under my body and the other above and said: 'I am frozen, and so cold that I am afraid to touch you for fear of hurting you.'

'Dear Mother, you need not be afraid of that.'

Immediately she put one hand on my breast and the other round my waist, her feet were under mine, and I pressed them so as to warm them, and she said: 'Oh my dear, see how my feet have warmed up at once because there is nothing between them and yours.'

'But,' I said, 'what is there to prevent you from warming yourself everywhere in the same way?'

'Nothing, if you are willing.'

I had turned round, and she had opened her nightdress, and I was on the point of doing the same when suddenly there were two violent blows on the door. I was terrified, and leaped straight out on one side of the bed and the Superior on the other. We listened and heard somebody tiptoeing back to the cell opposite. 'Oh,' I said, 'that is Sister Sainte-Thérèse. She must have seen you go along the corridor and come in here. She must have listened and overheard us. What will she say?' I was more dead than alive. 'Yes, it is she,' said the Superior angrily, 'I am sure it is, and I hope it will be a long time before she forgets her temerity.'

'Oh, dear Mother, don't do anything to her.'

'Suzanne, good-bye, good night, go back to bed and sleep well. I excuse you from early prayers. Now I am going to see this silly girl. Give me your hand . . .'

I held out a hand from one side of the bed to the other, she pulled my sleeve and kissed my arm all the way up from fingertips to shoulder, then she went out protesting that the impertinent girl who had dared to disturb her would not forget it in a hurry. I at once leaned over on the side of my bed nearer the door and listened: she went into Thérèse's room. I was tempted to get up and go and intervene between her and the Superior if the scene became violent, but I was so worried and upset that I preferred to stay in bed, but I did not sleep. I thought I should become the talk of the convent, and that the episode, which could not have been more simple, would be recounted in the most damning detail, and that it would be even worse here than at Longchamp, where I was accused of something I did not

understand; that our offence would come to the knowledge
of higher authorities and that our Superior would be dismissed and both of us be severely punished. But I continued to be all ears, and anxiously waited for our Mother
Superior to leave Sister Thérèse's room. Apparently the
matter needed a great deal of clearing up, for she stayed
there almost all night. How I pitied her, in her nightdress,
almost naked and numbed with anger and cold.

In the morning I very much wanted to take advantage of
the permission she had given me and stay in bed, but the
thought struck me that I ought to do nothing of the kind. I
dressed quickly and was first in the choir, and the Superior
and Sainte-Thérèse did not appear, which pleased me very
much, because firstly I should have found it difficult to face
that sister without embarrassment, and secondly, since she
had been allowed to absent herself from church, she had
presumably obtained from the Superior forgiveness which
would not have been given without conditions which
should reassure me. I had my suspicions.

Scarcely was the service over than the Superior sent for
me. I went to see her; she was still in bed and looked exhausted. She said: 'I have felt ill and have not slept. Sainte-
Thérèse is out of her mind, and if this happens again I shall
have her shut up.'

'Oh, dear Mother, don't ever do that.'

'It will depend on how she behaves; she has promised to
be better, and I am counting on that. And what about you,
dear Suzanne?'

'Very well, Reverend Mother.'

'Have you had any rest?'

'Very little.'

'I have been told that you were in church. Why didn't
you stay in your bed?'

'I should have felt wretched, and besides, I thought it was
better to . . .'

'No, it wouldn't have upset anybody. But I feel I want to
sleep for a while. I advise you to go off and do the same,
unless you would prefer to accept a place beside me.'

'Dear Mother, I am most grateful, but I am used to sleeping alone and could never sleep with anybody else.'

'Well, go along then. I shall not be down to dinner, but have it served here, and may not get up for the rest of the day. Later you will come back with a few others I have invited.'

'Will Sister Sainte-Thérèse be one of them?' I asked.

'No.'

'I am not sorry to hear that.'

'Why?'

'I don't know. It seems to me that I was afraid of meeting her.'

'Don't you worry about that, my dear. I can guarantee that she is more frightened of you than you need be of her.'

I left her and went to lie down. In the afternoon I went to the Superior's room, where I found quite a large gathering of the youngest and prettiest nuns in the convent; the others had paid their respects and departed. You, Sir, who know about painting, can take my word for it that it made a very pleasant picture to look at. Imagine a working party of ten or twelve, the youngest of whom might be fifteen and the oldest not yet twenty-three, a Superior of about forty, white, fresh and plump, sitting up in bed with two chins which she was wearing quite elegantly, arms as round as if they had been turned on a lathe, slender yet dimpled fingers, large black eyes, shining and tender, hardly ever fully open but half closed as though their owner found it rather tiring to open them, lips rosy-red and teeth as white as milk, lovely cheeks and a very handsome head half buried in a deep, soft pillow, her arms spread nonchalantly along her sides, with little cushions supporting each elbow. I was sitting on the edge of her bed doing nothing, but another nun was in an armchair with a little embroidery frame on her knees, while others sat near the windows, making lace. Some were sitting on the floor on cushions taken from the chairs, sewing, embroidering, unpicking embroideries or spinning on a little wheel. Some fair, some dark, they were all different but all beautiful, and their characters were as varied as their faces, for some were placid and others gay, others again were serious, melancholy or sad. Everybody was at work except myself, as I have said. It was not difficult to see who were friends, who meant nothing to each other or were enemies; the friends were either side by side or opposite each other, and while working they chatted and exchanged advice, looked furtively at each other and linked their fingers on the pretext of giving each other a pin, needle or scissors. The Superior continually ran her eye over them, reproved one for working too hard and another for not getting on, another for her indifference or another for being sad; she had the work brought to her and praised or criticized it, readjusted the headgear of one of them: 'This veil comes too far forward ... This linen hides too much of your face and we can't see enough of your cheeks ... These folds don't fall properly ...' And each one had her little penalty or little rewarding caress.

While all this was going on I heard a knock at the door, and I went. The Superior said: 'Sainte-Suzanne, you will come back, won't you?'

'Yes, Reverend Mother.'

'Don't forget, for I've something important to discuss with you.'

'I'll come straight back.'

It was poor Sainte-Thérèse. She stood there for a minute without saying anything, and so did I. At length I said: 'Dear Sister, am I the one you are vexed with?'

'Yes.'

'Then how can I help you?'

'I will tell you. I have incurred our dear Mother's displeasure. I thought she had forgiven me, and had some reason for thinking so, and yet you are all gathered together in her room without me and I am ordered to keep to mine.'

'Would you like to come in?'

'Yes.'

'Would you like me to ask her permission?'

'Yes.'

'Wait there, dear friend, and I'll go...'

'But really, will you speak to her for me?'

'Yes, of course, why shouldn't I promise you, and why shouldn't I do it after I have promised?'

'Ah,' she said, looking affectionately at me, 'I forgive her her preference for you, for you have all the attractions, the most beautiful soul and the most lovely body.'

I was delighted to be able to do her this small service. I went back in. One of the others had taken my place at the bedside and was leaning over with her elbow between the Superior's legs and showing her her work. The Superior, with half-closed eyes, was saying yes and no but hardly even looking, and she didn't notice me standing there at her side. But she quickly came out of her moment of dreaming. The nun who had taken my place gave it back to me and I sat down again; and then, bending over slightly towards the Superior who had sat up a little against her pillows, said nothing, but looked at her as though I had a favour to beg. 'Well,' she said, 'what is it? Tell me, what do you want? How can I refuse you anything?'

'Sister Sainte-Thérèse...'

'I understand. I am very disappointed in her, but if Sainte-Suzanne intercedes for her I forgive her. Go and tell her she can come in.'

I ran off. The poor little thing was waiting outside the door. I told her to go in, which she did, trembling and with downcast eyes. A long piece of muslin with a pattern pinned to it dropped out of her hand at the first step she took; I picked it up, took her by the arm and led her over to the Superior. She fell on her knees, took one of the Superior's hands and kissed it, sighing and weeping, then she took one of mine, joined it to the Superior's, and kissed them both. The Superior signed her to get up and go where she liked, and she did so. Some refreshments were served. The Superior rose. She did not sit down with us, but walked round the table, putting her hand on somebody's head and tipping it gently backwards and kissing her on the forehead, pulling up another one's collar and letting her hand linger while pausing to lean against the back of the chair, going on to a third and letting her hand stray over her or putting it on to her mouth, and she only tasted with her lips the things that had been served and passed them on to one or another. Having wandered round a while she stopped opposite me and looked at me with great tenderness and affection, but the others kept their eyes lowered as if afraid of inhibiting or distracting her, and especially Sister Sainte-Thérèse. When refreshments were over I sat down at the keyboard and accompanied two sisters who sang in an untrained way, but with taste, correctly and with good voices. I sang too and accompanied myself. The Superior was seated at the end of the instrument and seemed to take the greatest pleasure in listening and watching me. The rest just stood round listening or took up their work again. It was a delightful evening. Then everybody left.

I was leaving with the others, but the Superior stopped me. 'What is the time?' she asked.

'Nearly six.'

'Some of our advisory committee are coming. I have thought over what you told me about your leaving Longchamp and given them my opinion; they have approved and we have a proposal to make. It is impossible for us not to be successful, and if we are it will mean a little benefit to our house and will add to your comfort...'

At six the committee members arrived – the confidential ones in a religious house are always very decrepit and very elderly. I stood up and they took their seats, and the Superior said to me: 'Sister Sainte-Suzanne, didn't you tell me that you are indebted to Monsieur Manouri for the dowry paid for you here?'

'Yes, Reverend Mother.'

'So I was right, and the nuns of Longchamp are still in possession of the dowry you paid when you went there?'

'Yes, Reverend Mother.'

'They haven't returned any of it?'

'No, Reverend Mother.'

'Nor paid you any allowance?'

'No, Reverend Mother.'

'It's not right, and that is what I have told our committee, and they think as I do, namely that you have the right to bring an action against them so that either the dowry be returned to you for the benefit of this convent or that they pay you an income on it. What you have because of the interest Monsieur Manouri took in your fate has nothing to do with what the sisters of Longchamp owe you, and he did not provide your dowry in order to let them off.'

'Of course not, but the quickest way to find out is to write to him.'

'Obviously, but if his answer is what we hope, here are the proposals we have to make: we will undertake the suit against the convent of Longchamp, and our convent will meet the costs, which will not be very heavy because there is every likelihood that Monsieur Manouri will not refuse to take the responsibility for the affair; and if we win, the convent will have a half share with you of the lump sum or the income. What do you think, dear Sister? You don't answer, you are dreaming.'

'I am dreaming that the sisters of Longchamp have done me a great deal of harm, and I should be terribly upset if they presumed I was taking my revenge.'

'It is not a question of revenge, but of demanding what is your due.'

'But make a public exhibition of myself once again!'

'That is the least of the difficulties, for you will hardly appear in this business. And besides, our community is poor and that of Longchamp wealthy. You will be our bene-factress, at least for your lifetime, and we don't need a motive of that kind for being interested in your preserva-tion, we all love you...' And all the committee chimed in together: 'Who couldn't love her? She is perfection itself.'

'At any moment I may cease to be, and a new Superior might not have the same feelings about you as I do – oh no, she certainly wouldn't. You may have little indispositions or little needs, and it is very pleasant to possess a little sum one can dispose of for relieving one's own anxiety or helping others.'

'Dear Mothers,' I said to them all, 'these considerations are not to be ignored since you are kind enough to mention them, and there are others which touch me more closely, but there is no personal distaste I would not be ready to sacrifice for you. The only favour I would ask of you, Reverend Mother, is that nothing is begun before you have consulted Monsieur Manouri in my presence.'

'That is perfectly reasonable. Would you like to write to him yourself?'

'Just as you please, Reverend Mother.'

'You write to him then, and so as not to go all over this again – for I don't enjoy affairs of this kind, they bore me to death – write straight away.'

I was given pen, ink and paper, and thereupon I asked Monsieur Manouri to be so kind as to come to Arpajon as soon as his commitments allowed, for I once again needed his help and advice in a matter of some importance, etc. The assembled committee read and approved the letter, and it was sent off.

Monsieur Manouri came a few days later. The Superior explained what the matter was, and he was of our opinion without any hesitation; my scruples were dismissed as ludicrous and it was decided that the nuns of Longchamp should be summoned the very next day. And they were. So, whatever I felt about it, my name reappeared in memoranda, statements, hearings, together with details, suppositions, lies and all the calumnies that can blacken a creature in the eyes of her judges and make her odious to the general public. But, Sir, what right have lawyers to calumniate people just as they like? Is there no way of bringing the lawyers to justice? Had I been able to foresee all the bitterness that this affair would entail, I swear I would never have agreed to let it be initiated. They were careful to send copies of the pieces of evidence published against me to some of the nuns in our convent. They were constantly coming and asking me about horrible details which hadn't a particle of truth, and the more ignorance I showed the more they concluded I was guilty. Because I explained nothing, confessed nothing, denied everything, they thought it was all true, and smiled and made indirect allusions which were most offensive; they shrugged their shoulders at the idea of my innocence. I wept and was in despair.

But troubles never come singly. The time arrived for going to confession. I had already blamed myself for the first caresses the Superior had given me, and the confessor had very strongly forbidden me to lend myself to it any more. But how can you refuse things which give great pleasure to another person on whom you are totally dependent, things in which you can see no harm yourself?

As this confessor will play a big part in the rest of these memoirs I think it is right that you should know about him.

He is a Franciscan named Father Lemoine, aged not more than forty-five. He has one of the handsomest faces you could find; kind, serene, open, smiling, pleasant so long as he is not thinking about his looks, but when he is, his forehead becomes wrinkled, his brows pucker in a frown, his eyes are lowered and his whole bearing becomes austere. I don't know two men more different from each other than Father Lemoine at the altar and Father Lemoine in the parlour, alone or in company. Incidentally all people in religion are like that, and I have often caught myself, on the way to the grille, stopping dead, adjusting my veil or my headgear, composing my expression, my eyes, mouth, hands, arms, countenance, walk and adopting a bearing and factitious modesty which last for a longer or shorter time according to the people I have to talk to. Father Lemoine is tall and well built, gay and very charming when he forgets himself; he is a beautiful speaker and in his monastery he is thought of as a great theologian and in the world as a great preacher; his conversation is delightful. He is very well informed on all sorts of subjects quite remote from his calling, he has a lovely voice and is musical, with a knowledge of history and languages, and is a doctor of the Sorbonne. Although still young, he has risen through the principal ranks of his order. I think he is free from intrigue and ambition and he is popular with his colleagues. He had applied for the position of Superior of the house at Etampes because it was a quiet position in which he could devote himself free from distractions to the researches he had embarked upon, and this had been given him. The choice of a confessor is an important business for a nunnery, for it is advisable to be directed by an important and distinguished man. Everything was done to get Father Lemoine, and our convent did get him, at least once in a while.

The carriage was sent from the convent on the eve of Holy-days of Obligation, and he came. You should have seen the commotion produced in the whole community when he was expected, how jolly everyone was, how they shut themselves up to prepare the examination of their conscience, how they worked it so as to keep him as long as they possibly could.

It was the eve of Pentecost. He was expected. I was unsettled, the Superior noticed it and spoke to me about it. I did not conceal the reason for my anxiety, and she seemed more afraid than I was, although she did everything to hide it. She characterized Father Lemoine as a ridiculous person, laughed at my scruples, asked me whether Father Lemoine knew more about the innocence of her feelings and mine than our own consciences and if there was anything on mine. I said no. 'Very well, then,' she said, 'I am your Superior; you owe me obedience and I order you not to talk to him about such nonsense. It is pointless for you to go to confession if you only have silly little things like that to tell him.'

However, Father Lemoine arrived and I was preparing for confession while some of the more eager ones had seized him. My turn was approaching when the Superior came and drew me to one side and said: 'Sainte-Suzanne, I have thought over what you told me. Go back to your cell, I don't want you to go to confession today.'

'But why not, Reverend Mother? Tomorrow is a great day, a day of general communion. What do you suppose people will think if I am the only one not to come to the holy table?'

'Never mind, they can think what they like, but you will not go to confession.'

'Dear Mother, if it is true that you love me, don't inflict this mortification upon me, I beg you as a special favour.'

'No, no it can't be allowed – you would get me into some fusses with that man, and I don't want to have any.'

'No, Reverend Mother, I won't.'

'Then promise me ... No, it is useless, you will come to my room tomorrow morning and accuse yourself before me. You have committed no sin about which I cannot set your mind at rest and for which I cannot absolve you, and then you can take communion with the others. So go along.'

So I went away, and was in my cell, miserable, worried, unsettled and not knowing what line to take, whether to go to Father Lemoine in defiance of my Superior, to rely on her absolution next day and perform my devotions with the rest of the house, or whether to keep away from the sacraments whatever might be said. When she returned she had made her own confession and Father Lemoine had asked her why he had not seen me, and was I ill? I don't know what she had answered, but the upshot was that he was waiting for me then in the confessional. 'Go along then,' she said, 'since you have to, but promise me that you will keep quiet.' I hesitated, but she insisted. 'Oh, don't be silly,' she said, 'what wrong do you think there is in keeping quiet about what it was not wrong to do?'

'Then what is wrong with mentioning it?'

'Nothing, but it is awkward. Who knows what importance that man may attach to it? So promise me...' I still wavered, but in the end undertook to say nothing so long as he did not interrogate me; and I went.

I made my confession and then stopped speaking, but he did question me and I kept nothing back. He asked me a thousand strange questions which I still don't understand even now as I recall them. He treated me indulgently, but spoke of the Superior in terms which made me shudder, calling her outrageous, a libertine, a wicked nun, a pernicious woman, a corrupt soul, and enjoining me on pain of mortal sin never to be alone with her and to submit to none of her advances.

'But Father, she is my Superior, and she can come into my room or summon me to hers whenever she wishes.'

'I know, I know, and that is what distresses me. My dear child, God be praised who has preserved you until now. Without daring to explain myself in any more detail for fear of myself becoming an accomplice of your unworthy Superior and, with the poisonous words that would come from my mouth in spite of myself, withering a delicate flower that is only kept fresh and stainless until your age by the special protection of Providence, I order you to avoid your Superior, repel her advances, never go into her room alone, lock your door against her, especially at night, and if in spite of you she does come in, to get out of bed, go out into the corridor, call for help if need be, even go naked to the altar, fill the house with your screams and do everything that the love of God, the fear of evil-doing, the holiness of your vocation or your desire for salvation might suggest if Satan himself were to come and pursue you. Yes, my child, Satan, for it is in that form that I am compelled to show you your Superior: she is sunk in the abyss of crime and seeks to drag you down into it, and you would perhaps be there with her already if your very innocence had not filled her with awe and stopped her.' Then, raising his eyes to heaven, he cried: 'Oh God, continue to protect this child ... Say with me *Satana, vade retro, apage, Satana*. If this wretched woman questions you, tell her everything and repeat what I have just said, tell her it were better for her that she had never been born or that she had thrown herself into hell by a violent death.'

'But, Father, surely you heard her own confession, just now.'

He made no answer, but sighed deeply, put his arms

against one of the sides of the confessional and rested his head on them like a man overcome with grief, and he remained thus for a long time. I did not know what to think, and was all of a tremble, in an indescribable state of agitation and confusion. I was like a traveller walking in darkness between precipices invisible to him, and who was assailed on all sides by voices from below wailing: 'You are doomed!' Then he looked at me calmly but with affection and said: 'Are you in good health?'

'Yes, Father.'

'You would not be too upset by a sleepless night?'

'No, Father.'

'Very well, you will not go to bed tonight, but immediately after your meal go into the church and prostrate yourself before the altar and spend the night there in prayer. You do not know the danger you have been in, you must thank God for having kept you safe, and tomorrow you will go to the holy table with all the other sisters. The only penance I give you is to keep well away from your Superior and repel her poisonous advances. Go now, and I am going to join my prayers to yours. What a lot of anxiety you are going to give me! I can see all the consequences of the advice I am giving you, but I owe it to you and I owe it to myself. God is master, and we have only one law.'

I have only an imperfect recollection, Sir, of all he said. At present, when I am comparing what he said as I have just set it down for you with the terrifying impression it made on me at the time, I can find no comparison. But that is because as it is set down it is broken and disconnected, and many things are left out which I have not kept in my mind because I had no clear idea about them, and did not see, and still do not see, any significance in things to which he took the strongest exception. For example, what did he think was so strange about the scene at the keyboard? Are there not people on whom music makes the most violent impression? I myself have been told that certain tunes and modulations completely changed my facial expression; at such times I was quite beside myself and hardly knew what

I was doing, but I don't think I was any the less innocent for that. Why couldn't it have been the same with the Superior who, for all her quirks and caprices, was one of the most sensitive women in the world? She could never hear a pathetic story without bursting into tears, and when I told her my own story I reduced her to a pitiful state. Why didn't he make her sympathy a crime as well? And the scene at night, the end of which he was waiting for in mortal dread ... Decidedly this man is too severe.

Anyhow, I carried out to the letter what he had told me to do, the immediate result of which he had no doubt foreseen. I went straight from the confessional and prostrated myself before the altar. My mind was in a whirl of panic, and there I stayed until supper time. The Superior, anxious about what had happened to me, had sent for me and been told that I was in prayer. She had appeared several times at the entrance to choir, but I had pretended not to see her. The supper bell rang and I went to the refectory, hurried over my meal, and as soon as supper was over returned at once to the chapel, made no appearance at evening recreation and did not go up at the hour for retiring and going to bed. The Superior knew quite well where I was. Night was well advanced and all was quiet in the convent when she came down and took her place beside me. The picture the confessor had shown me of her inflamed my imagination, and I trembled, dared not look at her for fear of seeing a hideous face enveloped in flames, and said within myself: *'Satana, vade retro, apage, Satana.* My God, preserve me and banish this demon from me.'

She knelt down and prayed for some time, then said: 'Sainte-Suzanne, what are you doing here?'

'You can see, Madame.'

'Do you know what time it is?'

'Yes, Madame.'

'Why didn't you go back to your room at the proper time for retiring?'

'Because I was preparing myself to celebrate the great occasion tomorrow.'

'Were you proposing to spend the whole night here, then?'

'Yes, Madame.'

'Who gave you permission?'

'The confessor ordered me to.'

'The confessor cannot order anything against the rule of this house, and I order you to go back to bed.'

'Madame, this is the penance he has imposed.'

'You will do other tasks instead.'

'That is not for me to choose.'

'Come along, my child, the cold in the chapel at night will upset you. You can pray in your cell.'

Then she tried to take me by the hand, but I moved quickly away. 'You are avoiding me,' she said.

'Yes, Madame, I am.'

Emboldened by the sacredness of the place, the Divine Presence and the innocence of my own heart, I dared to look up at her, but hardly had I seen her before I uttered a shriek and ran round the choir like a mad thing, shouting: 'Get thee behind me, Satan!'

She did not follow me, but stayed where she was, and holding her arms out lovingly said in the most touching and gentle voice: 'What is upsetting you? Stop. I am not Satan, I am your Superior and your friend.'

I stopped, turned and looked at her again and saw that I had been terrified by a strange effect of my own imagination: her position in relation to the church lamp had been such that only her face and the tips of her fingers had been lit up, the rest was in shadow, and that had given her a weird appearance. I recovered somewhat and dropped into a stall. She came up and was about to sit in the neighbouring stall, but I stood up and went to the next stall down. And thus I moved on from stall to stall, and so did she, until the last one, and there I stopped and begged her to leave at least one empty space between herself and me.

'By all means,' she said.

We both sat down with one stall between us, and then

she began to speak: 'Could one learn from you, Sainte-Suzanne, where this fear of my presence comes from?'

'Dear Mother,' I said, 'forgive me. It isn't me, it's Father Lemoine. He depicted in the most terrible colours the affection you have for me and the caresses you give me, in which I myself see nothing wrong. He has ordered me to avoid you, never to go to your room again alone, to leave my own if you come, and he has represented you to me as a demon. I don't know what he hasn't said about it all.'

'So you told him?'

'No, dear Mother, but I could not refuse to answer his questions.'

'Am I all that horrible in your eyes?'

'No, dear Mother, I can't help being fond of you and appreciating all the value of your kindnesses to me, and asking you to go on with them. But I shall obey my spiritual director.'

'So you won't come to see me any more?'

'No, dear Mother.'

'You won't let me come to your room?'

'No, dear Mother.'

'You scorn my affection?'

'It will be very difficult to do because I was born with an affectionate nature and I like affection, but I must. I have promised my confessor and vowed to do so before the altar. If only I could convey to you the way he explains things. He is a pious and enlightened man, and what interest has he in showing me perils where they don't exist? In alienating a nun from her Superior? But perhaps he can discern in the most innocent acts on your part and mine seeds of inner corruption which he believes are already fully developed in you and fears you will develop in me. I don't deny that when I think over impressions I have sometimes felt ... Why, when I came back to my room after being with you, was I so upset and abstracted? Why could I neither pray nor get on with anything? Whence came a sort of lethargy I had never felt before? Why should I, who have never slept in the daytime, feel myself drifting off into slumber? I thought it must be some contagious illness which was beginning to take effect on me. But Father Lemoine sees it differently.'

'And how does he see it?'

'He sees all the blackness of crime, your certain damnation and mine approaching and, oh, all sorts of things.'

'Now look,' she said, 'this Father Lemoine of yours is a visionary, and this is not the first piece of vindictiveness I have had from him. I only have to get attached to somebody in an affectionate friendship for him to make a point of driving her out of her mind – he has nearly driven poor Sainte-Thérèse mad. I am beginning to get tired of it and I shall get rid of this man. In any case he lives ten leagues away and it is awkward to get him here and you can't have him when you want – but we can talk about that when we have more leisure. You don't want to go upstairs, then?'

'No, dear Mother, I ask you as a favour to allow me to spend all night here. If I failed in this duty I should not dare to draw near to the sacraments with the rest of the community. But will you take communion, dear Mother?'

'Of course.'

'But didn't Father Lemoine say anything to you?'

'No.'

'But how was that possible?'

'Because he was never in a position to discuss it with me. One only goes to confession to acknowledge one's sins, and I see no sin in being very fond of such a dear child as Sainte-Suzanne. If there were anything wrong about it, it would be that I concentrated upon her alone a sentiment that should be spread equally over all those who make up our community, but that is not entirely my responsibility, for I cannot help distinguishing merit where it exists and feeling specially attracted by it. I pray God to forgive me, but I cannot see how this Father Lemoine of yours can see my damnation all signed and sealed in such a natural preference which it is difficult to avoid. I try to work for everybody's happiness, but there are some whom I esteem and love more than others. That is all my crime as far as you are concerned. Sainte-Suzanne, do you think it is so serious?'

'No, dear Mother.'

'Very well then, dear child, let us say one more little prayer and leave.'

Once more I begged her to let me spend the night in the church, and she consented on condition that it should never happen again, and then went away.

I went over what she had said and asked God to enlighten me. I reflected and came to the conclusion that, when all is taken into account, although people might be of the same sex there could at any rate be some indecency in the way they expressed their friendship, and that Father Lemoine, himself an austere man, had perhaps exaggerated things, but that his advice to avoid the extreme familiarity of my Superior by exercising considerable reserve was a good one to follow, and I resolved to do so.

Next morning when the nuns came to choir they found me in my place. They all went up to the holy table, headed by the Superior, which finally convinced me of her innocence but did not make me change the attitude I had taken. And moreover I was far from feeling for her all the affection that she had for me. I could not help comparing her with my first Superior. What a difference! There was neither the same piety, nor the same seriousness, nor dignity, nor fervour, nor intelligence, nor sense of order.

Within the next few days two important things happened: one was that I won my suit against the nuns of Longchamp and they were sentenced to pay the convent of Sainte-Eutrope, where I was, a regular income in proportion to my dowry; the other was a change of confessor. The Superior herself informed me of the second.

But I no longer went to her room unless with somebody else, and she never came alone to mine. She still sought me out but I avoided her, she noticed it and reproached me. I don't know what was going on in her soul, but it must have been something most strange. She would get up in the night and wander about in the corridors, especially mine – I could hear her passing and repassing, stopping outside my door, moaning and sighing, and I shuddered and buried myself under the bedclothes. In the daytime, if I was walking or in the workroom or recreation room where I could see her, she would spend whole hours looking at me, watching my every movement. If I went downstairs I would find her at the bottom, and she would be waiting for me at the top when I went up again. One day she stopped me and began looking at me without saying a word, and the tears ran down her face; then she suddenly flung herself to the ground, and clinging to one of my knees with both hands said: 'Cruel Sister, ask for my life and I will give it to you, but don't avoid me, I couldn't go on living without you, my dearest...' Her condition filled me with pity, her eyes were lifeless and she had lost all her plumpness and bloom. She was my Superior and here she was at my feet, her head was on my knee which she was grasping. I held out my hands and she eagerly clutched them, kissed them and looked at me again. I raised her to her feet. She staggered and could hardly walk, and so I led her back to her cell. When her door was open she took me by the hand and gently tried to pull me in, but without speaking or looking at me.

'No,' I said, 'dear Mother, no. I have made a vow, and it is best for you and me. I am occupying too much space in your soul, which is that much lost to God, to whom you owe all.'

'Are you the one to blame me...?'

While I was speaking I was trying to get my hand away from hers.

'So you won't come in?'

'No, dear Mother, no.'

'You won't, Sainte-Suzanne? You don't know what the result may be, no, indeed you don't. It will kill me.'

These words produced exactly the opposite effect on me to the one she was aiming at, for I snatched my hand away and fled. She turned, watched me going for a few steps and then went into her cell, but left the door open and gave vent to the most heartrending wailing. I heard it and was filled with pity. For a moment I was not sure whether I ought to go on or go back, but some instinct of aversion made me go on, though not without feeling very distressed at the state I was leaving her in, for I am naturally sympathetic. I shut myself in my own room, where I was restless, didn't know what to do, walked up and down listless and worried, went out and came back. Eventually I went and knocked at the door of my neighbour Sainte-Thérèse. She was in the middle of an intimate conversation with another young nun, one of her friends, and I said: 'Dear Sister, I am sorry to interrupt you, but I do want just a word with you.' She went back with me into my room, and I said: 'I don't know what is wrong with Reverend Mother, she is very distressed, and if you went to see her you might cheer her up...' She didn't answer but, leaving her friend in her room, shut her door and hurried off to the Superior's.

But this woman's malady worsened from day to day. She became melancholy and serious; the gaiety which had never been absent since my arrival at the convent suddenly disappeared. Everything returned to the strictest discipline, the offices were conducted with fitting dignity, strangers were almost completely excluded from the parlour, nuns were not allowed in and out of each other's rooms, religious exercises were resumed with the utmost punctiliousness, there were no more parties in the Superior's room, no refreshments, the most trivial offences were severely punished. I was still sometimes asked to intercede, but I refused absolutely to beg for favours. The cause of this revolution was not unknown to anyone, and the older ones were not sorry, but the younger ones were in despair; they looked upon me with a jaundiced eye, but I ignored their ill-tempered reproaches.

The Superior, whom I could neither help nor keep myself from pitying, passed successively from melancholy to piety and from piety to frenzy. I will not follow her through these different stages, for it would involve me in endless detail – suffice it to say that in her first stage she sometimes sought me out and sometimes avoided me, sometimes treated us all, the others as well as me, with her customary kindness, but also sometimes passed suddenly to the most exaggerated severity, summoned us and sent us away, allowed time for leisure and cancelled her order a moment later, called us to choir and when everybody was obediently on the way the bell was tolled for complete seclusion. It is difficult to imagine the disorganization of the life we led; the whole day was spent in coming out of one's room and going back, taking up one's breviary and putting it down, going up and down the stairs, lowering and lifting one's veil. The night was interrupted almost as badly as the day.

Some of the nuns came to me and tried to give me to understand that if I were a little more accommodating and affectionate with the Superior everything would return to the normal (they ought to have said abnormal) order, but I sadly replied: 'I am sorry for you, but tell me plainly what I should do.' Some went away with lowered eyes and said not a word, others gave me advice that I could not possibly reconcile with our confessor's, I mean the one who had been dismissed, for we had not yet seen his successor.

The Superior no longer wandered about at night, but spent weeks on end without showing herself at offices, choir, refectory or recreation. She remained shut up in her room or wandered along the corridors or went down to the chapel, knocked at the doors of the nuns and said in pitiful tones: 'Sister So-and-So, pray for me, Sister So-and-So, pray for me...' Rumour spread that she was preparing for a public confession.

One day, when I was the first down to chapel, I saw a paper attached to the curtain of the grille; I went up to it and read: 'Dear Sisters, you are asked to pray for a nun who has strayed from her duties and wants to return to God.' I was tempted to pull the paper off and yet I left it there. A few days later there was another on which was written: 'Dear Sisters, you are invited to implore God's mercy on a nun who has acknowledged her misdeeds, and they are grievous...' Yet another day there was another invitation which read: 'Dear Sisters, you are implored to ask God to take away the despair of a nun who has lost all confidence in the divine mercy.'

All these invitations, in which the cruel vicissitudes of this soul in torment were made clear, saddened me profoundly. Once I remained rooted there in front of one of those notices, wondering what these misdeeds for which she was reproaching herself could be, what could be the reason for this woman's terrors, what crimes she could blame herself for. I went over the confessor's exclamations, I recalled his expressions and tried to find a meaning in them, but I could not, and remained lost in thought. A few nuns were watching me and talking among themselves, and unless I am mistaken they thought I was immediately threatened with the same terrors.

This unhappy Superior was never seen without lowered veil, she took no further part in the affairs of the house and spoke to nobody, but had frequent colloquies with the new director we had been given. He was a young Benedictine. I don't know whether he had imposed all the mortifications she practised – she fasted three days a week, she scourged herself, she heard offices in the lowest stall. We had to pass her door on the way to the church, and there we saw her lying prostrate with her face to the ground, and she only rose when everybody had gone. At night she went down in her nightgown, barefoot, and if Sainte-Thérèse or I met her by chance she turned away and pressed her face against the wall. One day I emerged from my cell and found her flat on the ground with her arms extended and face to the floor, and she said: 'Come on, come on and trample me underfoot. I don't deserve any other treatment.'

For months on end this illness went on, and the rest of the community had plenty of time to suffer from it and turn against me. I will not go once again into the unpleasantnesses undergone by a nun who is hated in her convent, you should know all about that by now. I gradually felt my distaste for my calling coming back. I confided this

distaste and my troubles to the new confessor. His name is
Dom Morel, a passionate man still under forty. He seemed
to listen attentively and with great interest, he wanted to
know the story of my life and made me go into the minut-
est details about my family, likes and dislikes, my character,
the convents in which I had lived and the one where I now
was, as well as what had passed between the Superior and
myself. I kept nothing from him. He did not seem to attach
the same importance as Father Lemoine to the behaviour
of the Superior towards me, for he scarcely bothered to
make more than a few remarks about that and treated the
matter as closed, whereas what concerned him most was my
innermost feelings about the religious life. As I opened out
about this, his trust in me made similar progress, and if I
confessed to him he confided in me about himself, and what
he told me about his own troubles tallied exactly with
mine; he had entered the religious life against his will, had
borne his situation with the same distaste, and was hardly
less deserving of pity than I was.

'But, my dear Sister,' he said, 'what can be done about it?
There is only one expedient left, and that is to make our
situation as little irksome as possible.' And then he gave me
the advice he followed himself, and it was wise: 'Even so,
you don't escape from sorrows but merely resolve to bear
them. People in the religious life are only happy insofar as
they make their crosses a merit in the eyes of God. Then
they find joy in them, they seek out mortifications, and the
more bitter and frequent they are the more proud they feel;
they have bartered their present happiness for happiness in
the hereafter, they are assured of the latter by deliberate
sacrifice of the former. When they have suffered much they
say to God: *Amplius, Domine*; Lord, still more ... and it is
a prayer that God seldom fails to hear. But though these
troubles are made for you and me just as for them, we
cannot promise ourselves the same reward, for we lack the
one thing that might give them value, resignation; and that
is a pity. Alas, how can I inspire in you a virtue you don't
possess any more than I do? And yet without it we run the

risk of being doomed in the life to come after being most wretched in this one. In the midst of penances we damn ourselves almost as certainly as worldly folk amid their pleasures; we deprive ourselves, and they indulge themselves, and after this life the same tortures await us. How dreadful is the condition of a nun or a priest who has no vocation! Yet it is ours and we cannot change it. We have been loaded with heavy chains which we are condemned to try ceaselessly to shake off, with no hope of breaking them; so, dear Sister, let us try to drag them after us. Go along now, I will come and see you again.'

He did come back a few days later, and I saw him in the parlour and examined him more closely. He finished confiding in me and I found a great number of circumstances in our lives which established between us many points of contact and similarity – indeed he had gone through almost the same domestic and religious persecutions. I did not perceive that the story of his revulsion was not at all calculated to dispel mine; yet that was the effect produced on me, and I believe that the tale of my revulsion produced the same effect upon him. And so it was that our similarity of character, together with that of the events in our lives, made us enjoy each other's company more as we saw more of each other. The story of certain moments in his life was that of mine, the story of his emotions was that of mine, the story of his soul was that of mine.

When we had thoroughly discussed ourselves we talked about the others as well, and above all about the Superior. His function as confessor made him very guarded, but nevertheless I read into what he said that that woman's present state of mind could not last, that she was fighting a losing battle against herself and that one of two things would happen: either she would soon go back to her first inclinations or go out of her mind. I was intensely curious to know more, for he might have enlightened me on questions I had asked myself and had never been able to answer, but I dared not interrogate him and merely ventured to ask him if he knew Father Lemoine.

'Yes I do, he is a man of merit, great merit.'

'One moment he was with us, the next he was not.'

'That is true.'

'Couldn't you tell me how that came about?'

'I should be sorry if that ever became known.'

'You can count on my discretion.'

'I think a letter of complaint was sent about him to the Archbishop.'

'Whatever could it have said?'

'That he lived too far from the convent and could not be available when required, that his moral standards were too austere, that there was some reason to suspect him of advanced views, that he sowed dissension in the convent and turned the nuns against their Superior.'

'Who told you that?'

'He did himself.'

'So you see him?'

'Oh yes, and he has sometimes spoken to me about you.'

'What did he say about me?'

'That you were very much to be pitied, that he could not imagine how you had stood up to all the trials you have been through, and that although he had only had occasion to speak to you two or three times, he didn't think you could ever adjust yourself to the religious life, and that he had in mind to...'

He stopped short, and I added: 'What had he in mind?'

Dom Morel replied: 'That is a confidential matter, and too much so for me to be free to go on...'

I did not insist, but merely added: 'It is true that it was Father Lemoine who turned me against my Superior.'

'And rightly.'

'Why?'

'Sister,' he said in a very serious tone, 'abide by his advice, and try as long as you live to remain ignorant of the reason.'

'But it seems to me that if I knew what the peril was I should be all the more careful to avoid it.'

'But perhaps it would work the other way.'

'You must have a very poor opinion of me.'

'I have the opinion I ought to have about your morals and innocence, but believe me there is such a thing as poisonous knowledge which you couldn't acquire without loss. It is your very innocence which filled your Superior with awe, and had you known she would have respected you less.'

'I don't understand.'

'All the better.'

'But how can the endearments and caresses of a woman be dangerous to another woman?'

No answer from Dom Morel.

'Am I not just the same as when I came here?'

No answer from Dom Morel.

'Wouldn't I have gone on being the same? Where is the evil in loving each other, saying so and showing it? It is so delightful!'

'That is true,' said Dom Morel, raising his eyes, which he had kept lowered while I was speaking.

'Is this so common in religious houses? My poor Mother Superior, what a state she has fallen into!'

'It is terrible, and I fear it will get worse. She was not cut out for her way of life, and this is what happens sooner or later when you go against the universal law of nature: this constraint deflects it into monstrous affections which are all the more violent because they have no firm foundation. She is a sort of maniac.'

'She is mad?'

'Yes she is, and she will become worse.'

'And do you think that that is the fate in store for any who are involved in a way of life for which they have no vocation?'

'No, not everybody. Some die first and others have a flexible character which adapts itself in the long run; some are kept going for a time by vague hopes.'

'But what hopes are there for a nun?'

'What hopes? First to have her vows annulled.'

'And if that one has gone?'

'That some day the doors will be found open, that mankind will recover from the folly of shutting up young and vigorous creatures in a tomb and abolish convents, that the house will catch fire, the walls collapse or somebody come to their rescue. All these theories go round and round in their heads, they talk about them, and when walking in the garden they find themselves glancing up to see if the walls are very high. In the cell they seize the railings of the grille and absent-mindedly give them a gentle shake, if there is a street below the window they watch it, if they hear somebody going past, their hearts beat faster, they sigh for some rescuer. If there is some commotion outside and the noise is heard inside the house they hope, they look forward to some illness which will bring a man near to them or take them away for a cure.'

'True, true, you can read into the depths of my heart. I have entertained such illusions, and I still do.'

'And when they lose them, for these healing mists which the heart throws round reason are sometimes blown away, then they see the full depth of their misery, they loathe themselves and others, they weep, moan, howl and feel despair overtaking them. Some rush and throw themselves at their Superior's feet and seek consolation, others bow down in their cells or before the altar and call on Heaven for succour, others rend their garments and tear their hair, others look for a deep well, high windows, a rope to hang themselves, and sometimes find what they want. Others, after long fretting, fall into a kind of apathy and become imbeciles for life, others, of frail and delicate constitution, fade away in languor, but there are yet others whose nervous systems break down and they go raving mad. The most fortunate are those in whom the same consoling illusions are ever being reborn and go on lulling them almost to the grave; their lives go by in successive phases of self-deception and despair.'

'And the most unhappy, apparently,' I added with a deep sigh, 'are those who go through all these states one after the other ... Oh, Father, how sorry I am to have heard you say all this!'

'Why?'

'I did not know myself, and now I do, and my illusions will not last so long. There are times...'

I was going on, but a nun came in, and then another, then a third, four, five, six, I don't know how many. Conversation became general, some watching the confessor, others listening in silence with lowered eyes, several were asking questions at the same time, and they were all in ecstasies about the wisdom of his answers. But I had retired into a corner and let myself drift into deep reverie. In the middle of these conversations in which each one was trying to show herself off and win the holy man's preference by displaying her best points, somebody could be heard coming slowly along, stopping now and again and sighing. They listened and whispered: 'It is, it's our Superior,' and then fell silent and sat in a circle. It was indeed. She came in, her veil falling down to her waist, her arms crossed over her breast, and her head bent. I was the first one she saw, and at once she took one hand out from under her veil, covered her eyes and turned away. With the other hand she dismissed us all, and we silently went away, leaving her alone with Dom Morel.

I can foresee, Sir, that you are going to have a bad opinion of me, but since I was not ashamed then of what I did why should I blush to admit it? And how can I omit from this story an event which very soon had a sequel? So let us say that I am of a very strange cast of mind: when things could inspire your respect or add to your sympathy I write well or ill, but with incredible speed and facility; I feel gay in heart, expressions come easily to me, I am easily moved to tears and I seem to feel your presence and see you there listening to me. But if on the other hand I am obliged to show myself to you in an unflattering light, I have difficulty in thinking, expressions escape me, my pen labours, even my handwriting is affected, and I only go on because I secretly flatter myself that you will skip these passages. Here comes one:

When all the sisters had departed ... 'Well, what did you do?' Can't you guess? No, you are too honourable for that. I went along on tiptoe and noiselessly took up my position outside the parlour door and listened to what was being said. That is very wrong, you will say ... Oh yes, of course it is, and that is what I told myself, and my emotion, the precautions I took so as not to be seen, the number of times I paused, the voice of my conscience urging me at each step to go back – all this left no doubt about it in my mind, yet curiosity was stronger, and I went. But if it is wrong to have gone to overhear the talk of two people who thought themselves alone, isn't it even worse to tell you what they said? This is one of those passages I am writing and deluding myself that you won't read. That is not true, but I have to persuade myself that it is.

The first words I heard after a long silence made my blood run cold. They were:

'Father, I am damned for ever ...'

I recovered and I listened; and the veil which until then had obscured the peril I had been in was just being torn asunder when somebody called my name. I had to go and I went, but alas! I had heard all too much. What a woman, Sir, what an abominable woman!

(Here the memoirs of Sister Suzanne become disconnected, and what follows is only notes for what apparently she meant to use in the rest of her tale. It seems that the Superior went mad, and the fragments I am about to transcribe must refer to her unhappy state.)

After this confession we had a few days of serenity. Gaiety returned to the community and I was paid compliments which I indignantly repudiated.

She no longer avoided me and could now look at me, and my presence no longer seemed to disturb her. My constant concern was to prevent her from seeing the revulsion she inspired in me now that through a fortunate or fatal curiosity I had learned to know her better.

Soon she became taciturn and only said yes or no, wandered about alone and refused to take food, her blood became overheated, she had a fever, and delirium followed the fever.

Alone in her bed she would see me, talk to me, ask me to go nearer and address me in the most affectionate terms. If she heard somebody walking in her room she would say: 'That's her going by, it's her step, I recognize it. Call her ... no, no, leave her alone.'

The strange thing was that she never made a mistake and took somebody else for me.

Bursts of laughter would be followed at once by floods of tears. The sisters stood round in silence, some of them weeping with her.

Suddenly she would say: 'I haven't been to church, I haven't prayed to God ... I must get out of bed and dress, help me to get dressed...' If anyone objected, she would go on: 'At any rate give me my breviary...' She was given it and she opened it and turned over the pages with one finger and went on turning even when there were no more to turn; but there was a wild look in her eyes.

One night she went down alone into the church. Some of the sisters followed her. She prostrated herself on the altar steps and began to moan and sigh and pray aloud, then she went out, but came back and said: 'Somebody go and find her, she is such a pure soul, such an innocent creature! And if she joined her prayers to mine...' Then, addressing the whole community and facing the empty stalls, she cried: 'Go away, go away all of you and let her stay alone with me. You are not worthy to go near her, and if your voices blended with hers your profane incense would corrupt the sweetness of hers before God. Go away, go away...' Then she exhorted me to ask Heaven's help and forgiveness. She saw God, the heavens seemed rent with lightnings, opening and rumbling above her head, angels descended in wrath and the eye of the Lord made her tremble. She rushed in all directions, burying herself in the darkest corners of the church, begging for mercy, pressing her face against the

ground until she came over drowsy, the dank coldness of
the place having affected her, and she was carried lifeless
back to her cell.

The next day she knew nothing about this terrible nocturnal scene, and kept saying: 'Where are our sisters? I
can't see anybody and am left alone in this building. They
have all forsaken me, Sainte-Thérèse too, and they were
right. As Sainte-Suzanne has gone I can go out and shall
not meet her ... Oh, supposing I met her! But she has
gone, hasn't she? She really has gone? Happy the convent
where she is! She will tell her new Superior everything;
what will she think of me? Is Sainte-Thérèse dead? I heard
the bell tolling all night. Poor girl, she is damned for all
eternity, and it is my fault, my fault! One day I shall meet
her face to face and what shall I say? What answer shall I
make? Alas for her! Alas for me!'

At another time she would say: 'Have our sisters come
back? Tell them I am very ill ... Lift up my pillow ...
Unlace me ... I can feel something weighing down on me
there ... My head is burning, take off my coif ... I want to
wash ... Bring some water, pour it out, go on pouring ...
They are white, but the stain on the soul is still there ... I
wish I were dead, I wish I had never been born, and then I
wouldn't have seen her!'

One morning she was found barefoot, in her nightgown,
shrieking and foaming at the mouth, running round and
round her cell with hands clapped over her ears, eyes shut
and body pressed tight against the wall ... 'Keep away from
the abyss; do you hear those cries? It is the infernal regions,
and out of that deep chasm there rise flames – I can see
them, and amid the flames I hear confused voices calling
me ... My God, have pity on me! ... Go quickly and ring the
bell, summon the whole community and tell them to pray
for me, and I will pray also ... But it is hardly light yet and
our sisters are still asleep ... I haven't shut my eyes all
night; I long for sleep but can find none.'

One of the sisters said: 'Madame, you are in some trouble,
let me share it, and that may help you.'

'Sister Agathe, listen, come here, come closer, closer still. They mustn't hear us. I am going to reveal everything, everything, but keep my secret ... Have you seen her?'

'Who, Madame?'

'Isn't it true that nobody has the same gentleness? How she walks! What decorum, what dignity, what modesty! ... Go and tell her that ... Oh no, don't say anything, don't go ... You couldn't get near her, for the angels of heaven keep her and watch over her – I have seen them, and if you saw them you would be afraid, as I was. Stay here ... If you did go what could you say? Think of something that would not make her blush.'

'But, Madame, suppose you consulted your confessor?'

'Yes, yes of course ... No, no, I know what he will say, I have heard so much of that from him ... What should I discuss with him? ... If only I could lose my memory! ... If I could go back into the void, or be born again! ... Don't call the confessor ... I would rather you read me the Passion of Our Lord Jesus Christ ... Read it ... I am beginning to breathe again ... One drop of His blood is enough to purify me ... See, it is gushing forth from His side ... Hold that sacred wound above my head ... His blood flows down over me, but will not stay there ... I am lost! ... Take that crucifix away from me ... No, bring it back.'

It was brought back and she held it tight in her arms, kissed it everywhere, then said: 'These are her eyes, this is her mouth; when shall I see her again? Sister Agathe, tell her I love her, let her know the state I am in and that I am dying.'

She was bled, she was given baths, but her malady seemed worsened by remedies. I dare not describe all the indecent things she did and said in her delirium. She kept on putting her hand to her forehead as though trying to drive away unwanted thoughts or visions – what visions I don't know. She buried her head in the bed and covered her face with her sheets. 'It is the tempter!' she cried, 'it is he! What a strange shape he has put on! Get some holy water and sprinkle it over me ... Stop, stop, he's gone now.'

She was soon put under restraint, but her prison was not guarded well enough to prevent her escaping one day. She had rent her clothes, and ran along the corridors stark naked, with only two ends of rope hanging from her arms and she was shouting: 'I am your Superior, and you have all taken an oath to obey me. You have imprisoned me, you wretches! This is the reward for all my kindness, you are offensive to me because I am too good, I shall not be so any more ... Fire! Murder! Stop thief! Help! Help me, Sister Thérèse ... Help me, Sister Suzanne...' But she was overpowered, and as she was being taken back into captivity she said: 'You are right, you are right, alas! I have gone mad, I can feel I have.'

Sometimes she seemed to be haunted by visions of different kinds of punishments, she saw women with ropes round their necks or hands tied behind their backs, she saw some with torches in their hands, she joined with those making a public confession, she thought she was being led to her death and addressed the executioner: 'I have deserved my doom, I have deserved it. If only this torment were the last. But an eternity! An eternity of flames!'

I am reporting nothing that is not accurate, and all the rest of the true facts I could add I either cannot recall or should blush to soil these pages with them.

After living on in this deplorable condition for several months she died. What a death, Sir! I saw it myself, I saw that terrible picture of despair and crime in its last hour; she thought she was surrounded by infernal spirits waiting to seize her soul, and she gasped: 'There they are! There they are!' and tried to fend them off to left and to right with a crucifix held in her hand, and she yelled and shouted: 'My God! My God!...' Sister Thérèse soon followed her, and we had a new Superior, elderly and full of ill-temper and superstition.

I am accused of casting spells over her predecessor; the Superior believes this and my troubles start all over again.

Similarly the new confessor is being persecuted by his own superiors, and he persuades me to escape from the convent.

My flight is planned. I go to the garden between eleven and midnight. Ropes are thrown over which I tie round me, but they break and I fall, my legs are grazed and I have a terrible bruise on the buttocks. A second, and then a third attempt and I am hoisted to the top of the wall and drop down on the other side. But what a shock! Instead of the post-chaise in which I expected to be welcomed, I found a miserable public cab. So there I was on the way to Paris with a young Benedictine. I soon realized from the indecent tone he took and the liberties he indulged in that he was keeping none of the conditions which had been stipulated, and then I regretted leaving my cell and felt the full horror of my situation.

Here I shall describe the scene in the cab. What a scene, and what a man! I scream and the cabby comes to my rescue. Violent set-to between the cabby and the monk.

I arrive in Paris. The cab draws up in a side street at a narrow doorway opening into a dismal and dirty alley. The landlady comes out to greet me and puts me on the top floor in a little room where I find the more or less essential things. I am visited by the woman who lives on the first floor. 'You are young and must be finding it dull, Mademoiselle. Come down to my place and you will find a pleasant company of men and women, not all as charming, but almost as young as you are. We talk, play cards, sing and dance, and have all kinds of fun. If you turn the heads of all our young men, I swear that our young ladies won't be jealous or upset. So come along, Mademoiselle...' The lady herself was older and her eyes were kindly, her voice was soft and her words very persuasive.

I spend two weeks in this establishment, exposed to all the importunities of my vile seducer and all the riotous scenes of a disorderly house, watching out all the time for an opportunity to escape.

At last one day I found it by chance; it was well into the night, and if I had been near my convent I would certainly have gone back there. I rush ahead without knowing where. I am accosted by men, and panic seizes me. Fainting with fatigue I collapse on the doorstep of a candle-maker's shop. I am picked up, and when I come to I find I am lying on a miserable mattress, with several people round me. I was asked who I was and I don't know what I answered. They gave me the servant of the house to escort me home and I took her arm and we set off. After a considerable walk the girl asked me: 'Mademoiselle, I suppose you do know where we are going?'

'No, my dear, to the workhouse, I suppose.'

'The workhouse? Have you got no home, then?'

'Alas, no.'

'What did you do to get yourself thrown out at this time of night? But we are at the door of Sainte-Catherine, let's see if we can make them open it. But in any case you need have no fear. You won't stay in the street, but sleep with me.'

So I go back to the candle-maker's. The servant has a shock when she sees my legs all grazed by the fall I had when I escaped from the convent. I spend the night there. Next evening I go back to Sainte-Catherine, where I stay for three days, after which I am told that I must either go to the Salpêtrière or take the first job I am offered.*

* Sainte-Catherine and the Salpêtrière. The first of these corresponded to a hostel that today might be run by the Y.W.C.A. or Salvation Army, at which one is only allowed to stay for a limited time. But the Salpêtrière, which still exists on what is now the Boulevard de l'Hôpital, south of the Seine and just beyond the Gare d'Austerlitz, was the place of detention for prostitutes and female vagrants. It was there that Manon Lescaut was imprisoned and from there that Des Grieux helped her to escape. – *Trans.*

What peril I was in at Sainte-Catherine from both men and women, for I have since learned that this is where the men about town and brothel-keepers go for fresh supplies! But approaching poverty lent no force to the crude suggestions to which I was exposed. I sold my clothes and got others more in keeping with my situation.

I took a job with a laundress, with whom I still am. I take in the work that has to be done and I do the ironing; it is a hard day's toil and I am not well fed nor do I have pleasant living and sleeping quarters, but on the other hand I am treated kindly. The husband is a cab driver, his wife is a little sharp-tongued, but good-hearted. I would be fairly satisfied with my lot if I could hope to enjoy it peacefully.

I have heard that the police have arrested my seducer and handed him over to his superiors. Poor man! He is more to be pitied than I am. His crime has made a stir, and you don't realize the cruelty with which religious orders punish offences giving rise to scandal: he will be confined in a cell for the rest of his life, and that is also the fate in store for me if I am recaptured, but he will live longer in such conditions than I should.

I am still in pain from my fall, my legs are swollen and I cannot walk a step. I work sitting down because it would hurt me to stand. And yet I dread the time when they are better, for what excuse should I then have for not going out, and what risks shall I not run if I do? But fortunately I still have some time ahead of me. My family, who must know I am in Paris, are certainly making the fullest investigations. I had resolved to invite Monsieur Manouri to come and see me in my garret, and I would have sought and followed his advice, but he had died.

I live in a state of continual alarm and am terrified of the slightest sound I hear in the house, on the stairs or in the street, I tremble like a leaf, I cannot hold myself up and my work drops out of my hands. Almost all my nights are sleepless, and if I do sleep it is only fitful dozing, and I talk, cry out, shout, and cannot imagine how people round me have not yet guessed my secret.

It seems that my escape is public knowledge, as I expected it would be One of my fellow-workers talked about it yesterday, adding disgusting details and most distressing comments. She was, fortunately, hanging damp washing on the line with her back to the lamp, and so my confusion could not be seen, but still my mistress noticed I was crying and asked: 'Marie, what is the matter?' 'Nothing,' I answered. 'What!' she went on, 'surely you are not soft enough to waste tears on a wicked nun with no morals and no religion, who falls in love with a horrible monk and runs away with him? You must have a lot of pity to spare. All she had to do was eat, drink, pray to God and sleep; she was very well off where she was, so why didn't she stay there? If she had been on her beam ends just three or four times in weather like this it would have reconciled her to her position...' I answered that the only troubles people really understood were their own. I should have been better advised to keep my mouth shut, for then she wouldn't have answered: 'Get along with you, she's a slut, and God will punish her.' At this I bent over my table and remained like that until my mistress said: 'But what are you dreaming about, Marie? The work isn't doing itself while you are dozing there.'

I have never had the spirit of the cloister, and that is clear enough from what I am doing now, but I have become accustomed in the monastic life to certain behaviour which I go through automatically. For example, if a bell happens to ring I either make the sign of the cross or kneel down. If somebody knocks on the door I say *Ave*. If I am asked a question I nearly always end my answer with yes or no, Reverend Mother or dear Sister. If a stranger approaches my arms fold themselves across my breast, and instead of curtseying I bow. My companions start laughing and think I am imitating a nun for a joke, but they cannot go on and

on making this mistake, and my absentmindedness will give
me away and be my undoing.

Sir, hasten to help me. You will doubtless say: tell me what
I can do for you. This is what you can do. My ambition is
not great, I should like a post as a lady's maid or house-
keeper or even an ordinary servant, so long as I could live in
obscurity in a place in the depths of the country with nice
people where there were not too many guests. The wages
are not important – just security, peace, bread and water.
Rest assured that they will be satisfied with my work. In my
father's home I learned how to work, and in the convent to
obey. I am young and of a very gentle disposition, and
when my legs are better I shall be more than strong enough
for my job. I can sew, spin, embroider and launder, and
when I was still in the world I mended my own lace, and I
shall soon pick that up again. I am not clumsy at anything
and nothing is beneath me. I have a voice and am musical,
and I can play well enough to entertain any mother who
would like me to, and I could even give lessons to her
children, but I should be afraid of betraying my identity by
these signs of a superior education. If I had to learn hair-
dressing I would quite like that, and I would take some
lessons and soon master this little skill. Sir, any bearable job
if possible, or just a job of any kind, that is all I ask. You
can answer for my morals, for in spite of appearances I have
morals and even piety. Oh Sir, all my woes would be at an
end and by now I should have nothing more to fear from
men had not God stopped me – that deep well at the bottom of the garden, how many times have I been there! If I
didn't throw myself in, it was because I was left entirely free
to do so. I do not know what fate has in store for me, but if
I am obliged some day to go back into a convent I cannot
answer for anything – there are wells everywhere. Sir, have
pity on me, and do not lay up for yourself lasting regrets.

P.S. I am overwhelmed with fatigue, surrounded by terrors,
and peace has deserted me. These memoirs, which I wrote

hurriedly, I have just re-read at leisure, and I have noticed that without the slightest intention I had shown myself in every line, certainly as unhappy as I was, but much more attractive than I am. Could it be that we think men are less affected by a picture of our troubles than by a portrait of our charms? And do we count on its being easier to seduce them than to touch their hearts? I have too little experience of them, and I have not studied them sufficiently to know. And yet supposing the Marquis, who is reputed to be the most delicate of men, were to persuade himself that I am addressing myself not to his charity but to his lust, what would he think of me? This thought worries me. In reality he would be quite mistaken if he ascribed to me in particular an instinct common to all my sex. I am a woman, and perhaps a bit coquettish, who can tell? But it is a result of our nature, and not of artifice on my part.

PENGUIN ONLINE

read about your favourite authors

•

investigate over 12,000 titles

•

browse our online magazine

•

enter one of our literary quizzes

•

win some fantastic prizes in our competitions

•

e-mail us with your comments and book reviews

•

instantly order any Penguin book

'To be recommended without reservation ... a rich and
rewarding online experience' *Internet Magazine*

www.penguin.com